THE STORY GIANT

THE STORY GIANT

BY
BRIAN PATTEN

HarperCollins*Publishers*

HarperCollins*Publishers*
77–85 Fulham Palace Road,
Hammersmith, London W6 8JB

www.**fire**and**water**.com

Published by HarperCollins*Publishers* 2001
1 3 5 7 9 8 6 4 2

Copyright © Brian Patten 2001

Woodcuts by Andrew Davidson of The Artworks

Brian Patten asserts the moral right to
be identified as the author of this work

A catalogue record for this book
is available from the British Library

ISBN 0 00 711941 0

Set in Granjon

Printed and bound in Great Britain by
The Bath Press, Bath

For Linda Cookson

And in memory of Adrian Henri

Part One

The light of imagination transcends decay

THE STORY GIANT

Around the Castle he had woven an illusion of ruins that blocked it from the sight of mortals. To anyone out on the moor, the Castle appeared no more than a jumble of ancient stones and a few tall, roofless walls overgrown with lichen and ivy. The Story Giant was all but invisible, and his voice was often mistaken for the wind blowing over the tumbled stones.

It was how the Story Giant wanted it, how it had always been. He had created illusion upon illusion, mixing the real and imagined till they were one and the same. He was from a time before the ancient pharaohs. He had been intelligent when people were little more than apes, and had come into existence whole, as he was now. The Story Giant had never experienced childhood, yet his food and drink were the stories told and dreamt by humankind from its infancy onward. He was the custodian of those stories, and his castle was their storehouse.

Before writing had existed it had been hard to keep track of the world's growing pool of knowledge and folklore. People forgot things.

But not stories; they remembered stories. Into even the simplest story they had learnt to pour their understanding of each other and of the world around them. And the giant had learnt to sip wisdom and information from the stories, like wine from a glass.

But there was one story the Story Giant did not know. For thousands of years he had tramped the earth, always believing it would turn up sooner or later, carved in runes on an ancient stone, or found among the pages of a forgotten book. But it never had. And only tonight had he finally realized its importance.

Now, the thought of not finding the story filled him with dread.

In a city called Patna in Northern India a young girl called Rani curled up on the lattice-patterned floor of a small iron balcony and fell asleep. The clamour of the rickshaws and human traffic below her carried on into the claustrophobic, marigold-scented night, but Rani heard nothing. Having worked all day and a good part of the night in the steamy laundry of a hotel in a wealthy part of the city, she was exhausted. She slept deeply, dreaming of a cool, far-away castle in a land of gentle rain.

Hasan El Sedeiry's father and mistress had been out most of the evening at an embassy dinner in Riyadh, and though he'd begged to stay up until their return the house-servants were set against it. They would not bend even the slightest against his father's wishes, and so here he was, high up in his little minaret-like bedroom looking out over the mosques to the towers that edged the far side of the city.

He turned on the television, which was usually forbidden at this hour of the night, but it was an old film about goblins and giants and he'd seen it several times before. Sighing, he turned the room's cooling system to a low setting so that its hum would not disturb him, and climbed into his bed.

Sometimes Betts Bergman found it difficult to sleep because of the red and blue neon lights that blinked on and off below the bedroom window of the Los Angeles apartment her mother rented. No matter how tightly she pulled the curtains some light managed to get through. Some nights it did not matter, but on other nights even the faintest glow was enough to keep her awake. Tonight was that kind of night. She switched on the bedside lamp, picked up a dog-eared book that had been a favourite when she'd been younger, and began reading. Ten minutes later she was asleep, the bedside lamp still on, her book on the pillow beside her, still open at an unfinished story about a giant.

Liam Brogan lay on his bunk bed in the converted fishing-trawler he and his father called home. The boat rocked almost imperceptibly as the incoming tide lifted it from the South Devon mud-flats where it was moored, and nudged its bow round to face the estuary mouth. Liam could hear the cry of owls and, less frequently, the barks of squabbling fox-cubs. The sounds were muted by beads of mist and the sea-fret that fell on to the woods and lay like a comforting blanket over his thoughts, most of which had to do with school, and a book of ghost-stories that had been confiscated from him during a maths lesson that afternoon.

The Story Giant woke and sniffed the air. Children had come again. He could smell four of them – two boys and two girls. They were puzzled, but not frightened, and he decided he would have no problem weaving them into a single, unifying dream.

But for the moment they were each still locked in their own private dream.

The one called Liam was in the Castle's north wing, staring out of the thick mullioned windows at the falling snow.

Another child was leaning on a window-sill, looking down into a courtyard where lemon trees glowed in bright sunlight and a faint breeze rattled the polished green leaves. Now and then she would close her eyes, smile, and breathe in the lemon-scented air without a care in the world.

The third child, Hasan, was in the library pulling out books with which he immediately grew bored. He did not bother to replace them, no doubt thinking that one of the servants would do that later.

There was another visitor somewhere, but the Giant could not yet locate her.

He put down the book he had been reading and stood uneasily, his bones brittle and stiff with age. He descended a broad stone staircase flanked by wooden banisters, sections of which had crumbled away, leaving only sharp iron railings standing like rows of warriors' spears.

He lumbered on, through corridors and rooms abandoned to the workings of woodworm and time, until finally he came to the Castle's massive entrance hall. He pushed open its iron-studded door and stared out upon the moor.

It was neither snowing nor sunny outside. There were no lemon trees, there was no sound of rattling leaves. Instead, the moorland stretched in sombre isolation from one horizon to another. He sniffed the night air. The smell of heather and all the varied scents of the night drifted on the wind. He imagined he could even smell the moonlight that covered the gorse and bracken with an imitation of frost. He breathed in deeply once again, wondering if tonight would be his last chance to gaze upon the mortal world.

For the Story Giant was dying. The process had begun some time ago, and tonight, for the first time, he sensed that it was nearing its end. With each snuffle of the badger and hoot of the owl, Death rode faster and faster through the night towards him. Ahead of him, Death sent his messengers, world-weariness and pain. The Giant was not dying in the same way as most mortals die. There was no fear for himself, no on-going fight to stave off the inevitable decline into darkness. Rather, there was the kind of curiosity someone might feel about a sealed room they had passed endlessly without seeing inside.

But the Story Giant did not want to die. He knew that he needed to continue – not for his own sake, but for the sake of the stories he had nursed and cherished down the centuries. It was not Death he feared, but the consequences of death. He had caused the stories to be reinvented over and over again. Each retelling and twist had kept them alive and vibrant. His fear lay in the knowledge that if he were to die the Castle would die with him, and the millions of stories it contained would perish for want of retelling.

For that reason alone it was imperative he lived on. He knew there was only one thing that could save him. Somewhere there was a story that could rescue him from Death. It was the single story he did not know. Without it oblivion beckoned. But what was it? And where? And how had it had managed to evade him over so many centuries?

The Story Giant closed his eyes. And as he did so, a faint hope began to stir. He thought of the four new children who had suddenly appeared – tonight, on the very night he had finally accepted that he and the castle faced extinction. Could their arrival be a kind of omen? Could it be that one of the children knew the story – the tale that would bring with it salvation?.

His mind soothed by the moorland scents and by this one hope, the Story Giant pulled shut the door and turned his back on the night. It was time to weave the children together.

He made for the library where the child Hasan was now asleep, his head resting on a pile of discarded books.

Liam turned from watching the falling snow and stood with his back to the window. From a corridor up ahead of him he heard a voice whisper, 'It's weaving time, Liam. It's weaving time.' He followed the whisper, his tread on the cold flagstones muted by the dust of moths and the snow blowing in through fissures in the Castle's dilapidated walls. The voice ceased the moment he arrived outside an improbably high door.

Standing at the window staring down at the lemon-trees had given Rani a thirst. She was convinced that somewhere in the Castle was a nice cool glass of lemonade just waiting for her to drink it. She set out to find it, and in a blink was standing outside an unusually tall door behind which she knew – absolutely knew – the lemonade was waiting.

Betts Bergman found herself in what she took to be a private theatre. There were several rows of seats and each seat could have accommodated two people with room to spare. Oil-lamps hung from the high ceiling, operated by a system of pulleys. The neglected stage was deep and square. Its threadbare curtains were imprinted with golden masks and hung half-open. On the edge of the stage, propped against a stack of old play-scripts, Betts found a note.

Unsurprisingly (she was surprised by nothing in her dreams) it read, 'Please go to the room with the tall door on the third floor.' Somehow she found she knew the way, but being a bad time-keeper in her waking life, she was the same in her dreams, and was late arriving. When she rapped on the door a deep, gentle voice like none she'd heard before said, 'Come in, Betts.'

Behind the door was a large private library. It was cluttered with old sofas and battered leather armchairs. Three of the walls were covered in book-shelves that reached up to a high, vaulted ceiling. More books were piled up on desks and tables. No corner was free of them. Contemporary paperbacks were jumbled up with old leather-bound volumes; pamphlets and comics jostled for space with beautifully illustrated editions of the rarest books.

A stocky, tough-looking boy with untidy curly hair, dressed in an old-fashioned duffel coat a few sizes too big for him, was standing staring sullenly at something – or someone – hidden from Betts' view by a decorative screen. Sitting in a chair beside him was a tubby boy with beautiful olive skin, yawning and managing to look both mesmerized and bored. To his right stood a dark-haired girl holding a glass of lemonade. She was younger than the others, small and fragile and dressed in a long purple dress over which she wore a threadbare pink cardigan.

Betts walked further into the room and saw the focus of their attention.

Sitting hunched beside the fire in a throne-like chair was what appeared to be a giant. He was not a giant in the huge, fairy-tale sense. There was nothing fearsome or monstrous about him. It was simply his size that startled Betts.

Because he was seated she could not judge his true height, but she guessed him to be somewhere between ten and eleven foot tall. He had a smooth high forehead and thick, flame-coloured hair. Though he was kindly looking, the skin on his cheeks was pitted and scarred, and his hands, which clutched the arm-rests of the chair, were knotted with age. Into the mantelpiece above the fire grate was carved an inscription that read: *The light of imagination transcends decay.*

It seemed the Giant had already been talking a little while, answering a question that had been asked before Betts had entered the room. He nodded, acknowledging Betts, then continued to speak.

'Usually I leave people who dream themselves into this place alone and they wake without knowing I exist,' he said. 'If I had done the same with you, you would all have wandered about this castle passing through each other as unaware as moths passing through shadows.'

'Then why didn't you leave us alone?' It was the rough-looking boy in the too-large duffel coat who'd spoken.

'Because never before have four such very different children arrived here simultaneously,' the Giant said. 'It is a unique event in the history of my Castle. Why, you have even defied the logic of time-zones to appear here as you have.'

The Giant told them a little of his history, reassuring the children that they had no need to fear him. Then he spoke about the missing story and its importance, and of his conviction that they were all, in some mysterious way, connected to it. 'It's something I feel deep in my bones. Otherwise, *why* would you be here?'

He gazed into the fire, silent for a while, his great hazel-coloured eyes fixed on the flames. When he looked up again his voice was distant and sad.

'You know stories from separate ends of the earth,' he said. 'Is it too much to hope that among them is the one I long to know?'

Betts stared at the Giant in amazement.

'You mean you've *no* idea what the story's about?' she asked.

'If I had the faintest idea I would have discovered it by now. Tonight might be my last chance to find it, and ...'

He stopped. The pain that had been plaguing him for months passed through him like a wave of splintered glass, then was gone again.

'And?' Betts prompted him, unaware of what he had just experienced.

'And I *need* to hear stories, I *need* to tell and share them. It is the reason I exist,' he said.

'But what if we don't know any stories?' Liam again, still sullen and defensive.

'Oh, but you do, all of you do. They are hidden in the depths of your conscious minds, and while you are here you will feel compelled to tell them. This is no ordinary place,' said the Story Giant. 'This whole castle is built out of Imagination. It is where stories take on lives of their own. It is where the fox learns to speak with a human tongue and where the rabbit learns cunning. It is here where barriers between logic and fantasy evaporate and one flows into the other.' The Giant looked from one child to the next. 'All this is done through the power of stories,' he said. 'Let me tell you a tale that might illustrate their mysterious nature.'

And so the story-telling began.

THE FIRST STORY

'ONCE UPON A TIME,' SAID THE GIANT, 'A YOUNG EXPLORER found himself the guest of an ancient tribe in a remote area of Central Africa. Each night when the tribe gathered to eat and drink and tell stories the explorer joined them. No one from the outside world had recorded the tribe's stories, which stretched back to the most primitive of times, and the young explorer felt himself to be in a unique position.

'After exchanging greetings and sharing food, the village elder, a man of about seventy, began telling one of the tribe's favourite stories. It was one of the oldest tales known to the tribe, and concerned a lion that whispered advice into a man's ear.

'The explorer recorded this and many other stories. He was very pleased with himself, and when he returned home he boasted over and over again about the wonderful stories he had discovered. Among the people he boasted to was an older explorer, who asked him, "What was your favourite story?"

'The young explorer replied that his favourite had been a story about a lion whispering advice into a man's ear. "The story is unique," he said. "No other explorer has recorded the tribe's stories."

'"I too have just come back from a long journey," said the older man. He described how he had spent his time wrapped in furs, shivering on the edge of a bleak, icy desert a world away from the humid, life-buzzing jungle of his young colleague. He explained that he too had come back with a collection of stories that the tribe he'd visited considered unique to its own culture.

'"And which one was your favourite?" asked the younger explorer.

'"It was a story about a lion whispering advice into a man's ear," said the older man.'

'One of the tribes must have got the story from somewhere else,' said Hasan.

'But how?' asked the Giant. 'Neither of the tribes had ever travelled. They were separated by thousands and thousands of miles, by mountains and oceans and deserts. Both countries were land-locked, and both said their story was old even before the invention of boats, let alone more modern forms of transport.'

'Then how did they know the same story?' persisted Hasan.

'I believe the story was old before either tribe existed,' said the Giant, 'and that the explorers had simply been talking to different branches of the same tribe.'

'Which is?'

'Humankind.'

'Neat,' said Betts. She had been standing in a corner, propped up against a bookcase, listening with one ear while flicking through a book. 'Is that the point of your story, then?' she asked. 'That we are all different branches of the same tribe?'

'I don't think there's ever just one point or meaning to any story,' said the Giant. 'Just as there is no right way or wrong way to interpret them.'

Hasan felt irritated with Betts for interrupting what he thought was his own private conversation with the Giant: after all, he had been in the library first. 'I've got a story as well,' he said.

'Then by all means tell it,' said the Giant.

Hasan hesitated. 'But what if it's not the one you are looking for? Will I be sent away from here?

'Of course not,' said the Giant.

Still Hasan hesitated. He enjoyed being the centre of attention, but was uncomfortable in such an informal atmosphere among a group of strangers. He was the son of a strict and powerful man, used to doing exactly what was expected of him, and what was expected of him was being in bed asleep, not sharing other people's dreams. He suddenly noticed he wasn't even wearing his pyjamas any longer, but was in his day clothes. It was all rather muddling. He was afraid of being rejected by these people, even if they were only dream people. For a year now he had lived with this fear of rejection, of being spurned and left alone. Ever since ... but he could not bear to think about the tragedy that had befallen him. He knew he would burst out crying if he did. And showing his emotions was another thing Hasan found difficult.

'But if I did have to leave here, what would happen?' he persisted.

'You would simply wake up in your own bed and remember us all only as the dream we are,' said the Giant. 'No harm would come to you.'

This reassured Hasan. 'I'm only telling my story because it's funny,' he said, feeling he was regaining control of his strange situation. 'It doesn't *mean* anything.'

And so he told his story.

THE MAN WHO KILLED TWO
THIEVES WITH A CHICKEN

A FARMER OVERHEARD TWO NOTORIOUS THIEVES PLOTTING
to rob him that very afternoon. Having nothing to rely on but
his wits, he quickly rushed home and said to his wife, 'We're
about to be robbed. Cook a meal of lamb and apricots, but
don't let anyone see you prepare it. As soon as you're done,
hide it away. When the thieves I'm expecting arrive, tell them
I'm out in the fields with something precious. The moment
they set off to find me lay the dinner on the table with two
extra places.'

After giving his wife these strange instructions the farmer
took one of the two chickens he kept in a cage in the yard, tied

it up in a bag, and rushed off into his fields. Sure enough, the thieves turned up a while later and his wife, who by then had cooked and hidden the meal, sent them off after him.

When the farmer saw the thieves approaching he didn't give them a moment to think. 'Well timed!' he called. 'I was just about to stop work and have a meal. I must send a messenger to my wife to tell her you'll be joining us.'

'What messenger?' asked the puzzled thieves, looking about them. 'You're quite alone here.'

'Alone? I'm most certainly not alone,' said the farmer. 'I have this magic chicken with me.' He pulled the chicken from the bag, held it to the ground by its neck, and instructed it: 'Go and tell my wife to prepare a meal of lamb and apricots for our honoured guests.'

The moment he let the frightened chicken go it scrambled off, and with a great clucking and flapping of wings vanished over a hedgerow.

The thieves thought the farmer quite mad, but when he led them back to the farmhouse they were astonished. There was the meal, exactly like the one he had ordered, waiting for them.

The thieves were burning with curiosity about the chicken and after the meal they asked to see it.

'I'll fetch it right away,' said the farmer. A few moments

later he returned with his second chicken, which to the thieves looked pretty much like the first one.

'Don't you think it's wonderful having such a fine chicken?' he asked, dangling it enticingly before their eyes. 'Why, sometimes it even lays golden eggs.'

'Aren't you afraid of it being stolen?' asked the thieves.

'Not in the slightest,' said the farmer. 'Anyone who tried to steal this magic chicken would drop down dead immediately.'

'Then how much do you want for it?' they asked.

'You can have this one as a gift,' said the farmer, handing it across to them. 'I'm sure I can find another sooner or later.'

The thieves couldn't believe what a fool the man was. They thanked him and took the chicken off with them, convinced it was worth a fortune. On their way back to town the thieves started to mistrust one another, each man wanting to have the chicken to himself.

'I'll hold it.'

'No, I'll hold it.'

'Give it me.'

'It's mine.'

And so on.

They grew furious, drew knives and began fighting.

Soon one of the thieves lay dead, stabbed through the neck, and the other lay groaning on the earth, badly wounded. 'Go and tell the people in my village I'm dying and need help,' croaked the surviving thief, taking the chicken from the bag and releasing it. The bird went scurrying off in a panic.

The mortally-wounded thief waited for the chicken to return with help, but of course it never came back, and all the time blood was running from his wound like water from a tap. Before long he, too, died.

And that's how the farmer killed two thieves with a chicken.

—⁓—

When he finished the story Hasan grinned at the others. 'Imagine! Killing two thieves with a *chicken*.'

Maybe it was the way he told his story, but no one else seemed to think it was quite as funny as he did, and when Betts jumped in and began discussing what, if anything, it meant, Hasan told her she was being ridiculous. But Betts was keen to find a meaning, if only to impress the Story Giant. 'It's about how greed can blind you,' she said. 'It's about how it can make you do stupid things. Can you think of anything more silly than the idea of an intelligent chicken? What do you think, Liam?'

Liam could think of a lot of things sillier than a chicken – half the population of the world, for example. But he simply shrugged and nodded in agreement. If anyone other than Betts had asked him, he would have said he couldn't care less, but he liked the way Betts looked.

'See, Liam agrees with me,' said Betts.

But Hasan was insulted that his story had not gone down as well as he'd hoped, and soon a squabble had broken out between him and Betts.

Liam watched them, saying nothing. Dressed in black jeans and a white T-shirt over which she wore a bottle-green jacket Betts was exactly how he imagined Americans should look. But perhaps she wasn't so cool after all, he thought. He couldn't see the point in her arguing with Hasan, who was so much younger than her.

The Giant couldn't see the point of them arguing either. 'Stop standing on each other's tongues,' he admonished. 'That's the way wars begin.'

HOW WARS BEGIN

THREE CHILDREN FROM DIFFERENT COUNTRIES FOUND SOME
money outside a shop and decided to go in and buy something.

The first boy was Greek. He said, 'I'd like some *zacharota*.'

The second boy was from Italy. He said they should all buy
something he called *dolci* with the money. The third boy who
was from France insisted they had *bonbons*.

Within minutes they'd started to fight. From being the best
of friends they'd suddenly become the bitterest of enemies.
They were squabbling and pushing one another all over the
shop and arguing about what to spend the money on.

When the shopkeeper finally separated them he put a bag

of sweets on the counter and said, 'Next time, before you start fighting, I suggest you find out what it is you are fighting over first.'

—ɱ—

'Is that it? asked Hasan. 'The whole story? I don't understand it.' 'They all wanted the same thing,' said the Giant. 'They were all asking for sweets in their own language, but they didn't know it. Most stories are to do with conflicts of one kind or another,' he explained. 'Whether it's a conflict between armies or children in a sweetshop, or even between our own emotions. It is often what makes us want to read and hear stories – we're all keen to know the outcome of whatever the conflict is. I'll tell another story,' said the Giant, 'this time about a different kind of conflict.'

THE LITTLE MONSTER THAT GREW AND GREW

A SOLDIER RETURNING HOME ALONE FROM A GREAT BATTLE found a monster blocking his path. It wasn't much of a monster. In fact it was quite pathetic. It was small, its claws were blunt, and most of its teeth were missing. The soldier had won all the battles he had ever been in and was considered something of a hero.

He decided he would deal with the rather feeble-looking monster there and then.

He had run out of bullets, so using his rifle as a club he brought the creature to the ground with a single blow. Then he stepped over it and continued along the path. Within minutes the monster was in front of him again, only now it looked slightly larger and its teeth and claws were a bit sharper.

Once again he hit the monster, but this time it took several blows to bring it down. Again he stepped over it, and again, a few minutes later, the monster appeared before him, bigger than ever.

The third time, no matter how much he hit the monster it would not go down. It grew larger and more ferocious with each blow the soldier aimed at it. Defeated, the soldier fled back down the path, with the monster chasing after him. Yet by the time it arrived at the spot where he'd first seen it, the monster had returned to its original size.

When another traveller appeared on the path the soldier stopped him and warned him of what had happened.

'Maybe we can fight it together,' he suggested, 'then we will overcome it.'

'Let's just leave the feeble little thing where it is,' said the traveller. 'If you pick a quarrel with something unpleasant when you don't really have to, then it simply grows more unpleasant. Let's just leave it alone.'

And so they did. They walked around the toothless little monster and continued unhindered along the path.

'Well, I guess even Hasan would agree there's a meaning in that story,' said Betts. 'The soldier became obsessed with the little monster, who stands for our worries, but if he'd not tried to fight it, it wouldn't have grown, and he wouldn't have had a problem in the first place.'

So far the Indian girl, Rani, had said nothing. She'd enjoyed being in the Castle and in the Giant's presence so much that she'd hardly given the other children a moment's thought. With its windows looking out onto the rainy moorland and its hundreds of polished shelves and countless books, the library was the most wonderful room she'd ever been inside.

When she did begin watching the older children, the first thing she noticed was how much richer they seemed in comparison to herself. Liam was stocky and strong; Hasan verged on being fat and Betts, for all her slimness, glowed with health. Although Liam and Betts would have disagreed, she imagined them as all coming from fabulously wealthy homes.

How different their worlds must be to hers!

She wondered if they could imagine the terrible stream of life that flowed daily through her home city – the small boy without hands who clip-clopped along the broken pavements with blocks of wood tied to his arms and who sounded for all the world like a horse, or the skeletal old rickshaw drivers, almost too weak to work, who slept day-long under the dusty trees. And there were those who were even worse off, men who could easily be mistaken for bundles of rags, men whom even the beggars scorned.

Rani's parents worked as servants, but although she owned little more than the clothes she stood in, she'd had more education than most children of her caste, and the thing she was most proud of was her reading. Not even her parents could manage as well as she. Her favourite reading by far was a simplified version of a book called the *Panchatantra*. She was determined to tell one of the stories from it.

She turned from the window she had been gazing out of, and taking a deep breath, faced into the room and said, 'I too can tell a story.'

Hasan, Liam and Betts were so surprised to hear her speak that their conversations froze in mid-sentence.

Encouraged by the way the Giant smiled at her, Rani hurried across the library and, smoothing down her dress, dropped down beside the fire at his feet.

'Yes, I can tell one. It is from our very famous book, the *Panchatantra*.'

'The what?' Betts looked down at the young Indian girl, amused by her enthusiasm.

'The *Panchatantra*. It is one of the great, great books of Indian literature. It is our masterpiece,' Rani said with pride.

With her delicate hand she beckoned the other children to sit beside her, for that's how stories were told, she knew, sitting and sharing in a circle.

'It contains the best stories in the world,' she said when they'd joined her.

'What about our stories?' asked Hasan. 'Aren't ours as good?'

'Tell us, Rani,' said the Giant. 'And Hasan, hush.'

'Well,' said Rani, 'in the last story, the soldier is returning home from a war, but in mine a poor man is wondering what the point of wars might be.'

THE TRAMP AND THE OUTCOME
OF WAR

A TRAMP HAD BEEN WANDERING LOST FOR WEEKS THROUGH a strange country that had been devastated by war. The war had been over for many years, but it had been so terrible that neither the land nor the population had recovered. Crops had been burned, once-fresh streams had been polluted, and the poor people had fled their homes taking everything they could carry with them. There was nothing for the tramp to eat or drink except the grubs he found under stones and the dew he licked from the grass at dawn. He was going mad with thirst and hunger and knew he would soon die unless he found food.

He had no idea why there had been a war. It was something he brooded over simply to help keep his mind off hunger. Every time his stomach rumbled, every time his lips cracked, he tried to think instead about the reason behind the war.

Wandering beside a small wood one day he heard a noise that disturbed him. Frightened, he crouched in the tangled roots of a giant oak tree and listened. *Thump-a-rump-rump, thump-a-rump-rump.*

The sound was repeated over and over again, and seemed to be coming from the far side of the wood.

The tramp edged his way slowly and carefully through the wood to investigate the noise. He was amazed at what he found on the other side.

The sound was being made by the seed heads of poppies being blown against the skin of an old war-drum. He had discovered the very place where the last of the country's great battles had been fought. And on this battlefield, among the worm-eaten butts of rifles and the skeletons of soldiers, was a wonderful sight.

There were apple trees and plum trees, pear trees and cherry trees, wild asparagus, and all manner of strange fruit and vegetables.

When the two armies had fallen, the fruit and other foods

they'd carried with them into war had rotted into the earth. The soil had been nourished by the decomposing bodies of the dead, and in time an orchard had sprung up among the ragged skeletons.

The tramp sat on the old war-drum and began eating a delicious plum.

'I may never discover the reason for the war,' he thought to himself, 'but the outcome is obvious. The end result of all this carnage and misery has been to feed a single tramp.'

The Giant was delighted that Rani, the most timid of the children, had suddenly blossomed. He knew the story already – it would have been too much to hope that his unknown tale could turn up so quickly.

He remembered back to when he'd first heard it, when the world had seemed almost new to him. He'd lived elsewhere then. In Kashmir, in a remote region of snow-capped mountains near a tribe that – because in those days he had not been so expert at concealing himself – had spotted him from time to time. They'd called him the Yeti, and thought him still there.

He had heard a very different version of the story back in those days. He tried to remember exactly how long ago it had been, alarmed at how moth-eaten his memory was becoming.

Had it been two – or even three thousand years ago? Whichever, the story had existed before then, even before written language as the world now knew it had been invented. His second memory of the story was seeing a Himalayan priest copying it down from a local tribesman. And how long ago had that been? Two or three hundred years before the birth of Christ? About that. Copying it had been a laborious task for the priest. The poor peasant had had a stutter.

And had it been only eleven centuries ago that he himself had passed the story on to a travelling scholar, some of whose texts still existed in Islamic museums to this day? The man had written in Sanskrit, an ancient language the Giant loved. And now here was the same story again, tripping lightly off a child's tongue, mangled, simplified, but recognizable all the same.

Rani telling her story re-affirmed for him his belief that the Castle he had created was indeed a special place. If children like Rani were not able to tell their stories, how would any stories survive? Without re-telling they would stagnate and die, or be entombed forever in a forgotten language. All things perish if they are left unnourished, he thought: stories without retelling, humans without love.

His delight in hearing the story again lifted his spirits, and he began to remember some of his own favourite tales. There were four in particular that shone in his imagination. He cleared his throat.

'I've four small jewels to share with you,' he announced. He closed his eyes, and resting his head back in the chair he addressed the room.

THE DIFFERENCE BETWEEN HEAVEN AND HELL

A YOUNG PANDA WAS SITTING UNDER A TREE CHEWING A bamboo shoot. It was a very inquisitive panda and like many very young creatures was always asking questions that were almost impossible to answer. Questions such as, 'Why is water wet?' and 'Why does fire burn us?'

One day it wondered what the difference was between Heaven and Hell, and because there was no one around to ask, it decided to find out for itself.

The young panda went to Hell first. It was like a gigantic café, full of round tables. At the tables were groups of pandas, snarling and screaming at each other across bowls of the most delicious bamboo shoots imaginable. In their paws they held chopsticks so long they found it impossible to feed themselves. Whenever they tried to pick up some food all they managed to do was poke each other in the eye. They were all starving and miserable.

Next the young panda visited Heaven to see what that place was like. It was surprised to see the same tables, and the same bowls of delicious bamboo shoots. These pandas also had very long chopsticks, but instead of looking miserable they were all smiling and licking their lips. They were having the most wonderful time imaginable, for instead of trying to feed themselves, which was impossible with such long chopsticks, they were feeding each other.

When it returned home the young panda decided Heaven and Hell looked pretty much the same, and that selfish pandas created their own Hell, and generous pandas created their own Heaven.

WHEN IMMORTALITY WAS LOST

DIFFERENT CREATURES HAVE ENDED UP LIVING THE WAY they do because of something that's happened in their past. The dove, for example, leads a comfortable enough life in a dove-cote, being fed seed and coming and going at will. Presumably this is because it was so helpful to Noah when he was on the Ark.

Other creatures didn't have such good luck in the past. Take the owl, the mole, the frog and the moth. Once they had lived together in a large orchard and wanted for nothing. Then one night a traveller came asking for shelter, and they offered him the use of a silver tent they kept for guests down by the river. Now, this guest was rather special, for with him he carried a jar that contained the Elixir of Life – immortality itself.

Some say the stranger was an angel, others are not so sure. Whichever way it was, he was a restless sleeper and that night, without knowing it, he knocked his precious jar into the river, and immortality was lost forever.

In the morning everyone was horrified to find the jar gone. Not knowing it had been carried away by the river, they all set about searching for it. The owl searched amongst moss-quiet ruins and in gloomy woods. The mole burrowed under the earth. The frog looked down dank wells and under stones. The moth searched in cupboards, looking up the sleeves of suits and in the folds of dresses. It even searched for the Elixir of Life in flames. None of them ever found it. But they still live the same way today; they are still searching.

SUPREMACY

ONE PERFECTLY CLEAR NIGHT A YOUNG GLOW-WORM crawled from a crevice in the vineyard wall and saw the stars for the first time. Naturally, it mistook them for glow-worms like itself.

'I never knew there were so many of us!' it thought. It sat staring at the stars the whole night long and when dawn came and the stars vanished it thought itself the sole survivor.

Then the sun rose, and the glow-worm retreated back into its crevice and peered out in even greater astonishment, for it believed that the sun was an even bigger glow-worm. It concluded that of all living things, glow-worms were supreme.

A man who had been studying the glow-worm smiled to

himself, thinking how deluded the little insect was. 'But then, how can something so insignificant know that it is Man who is the supreme life-force on the planet?' he thought.

He reached into the crevice to pick out the glow-worm and as he did so, he pricked his finger on a thorn. A fatal microbe entered the tiny wound and as it multiplied and went rushing towards his heart, it thought, 'How deluded the man is, to think himself as powerful as a microbe!'

JOHN AND PAUL

A MAN HEARD A RUMOUR THAT DEATH WAS COMING TO THE town in which he lived to search for a man called John. He was terrified that it might be him Death was after, for his name was John. Of course there were lots of men called John in the town, but he decided to take no chances. Within an hour of hearing the rumour he packed his bags and set off for a distant town, where he took up lodgings above a café in a small out-of-the-way street and changed his name to Paul.

The moment he'd settled in, he went down to the café and ordered food. He was hardly seated before Death came and sat at a table beside him.

'Aren't you supposed to be in a different town tonight?' the man asked.

'Yes,' said Death, 'but I've one more call to make here first.'

'And who might you be looking for?' asked the man.

'For someone called Paul,' said Death. 'I believe he has just arrived here from another town.'

The children found the Giant's last three stories impossibly sad. Instinctively, they understood the relevance of the stories to him, for they were all, in one way or other, about dying.

As the night progressed so the Giant's preoccupation with the consequences of not finding the missing story grew. He tried his best to hide his fear from the children, not wanting to upset them. But it was not possible to conceal entirely the enormity of his plight. Resting on the arms of his chair, his great hands trembled slightly, the veins twitching as he tried to accommodate the pain that came and went, flashing on and off like the beacon of a lighthouse on the edge of a dark, unforgiving ocean.

Rani and Hasan had been sitting apart from Betts and Liam, whispering and occasionally looking over at the Giant, obviously discussing him. It was not the missing story that preoccupied them, but something else. Eventually, they came and stood beside his chair where, egged on by Hasan, Rani asked, 'Are you a real giant?'

The Story Giant screwed up his face in a show of mock concentration and said, 'Well now, Rani, let me think about it. I am over three feet taller than the tallest human being who has ever lived – does that make me a real giant?'

'But in fairy-tales ...'

'In fairy-tales we are nasty pieces of work, aren't we?'

'You *are* much taller in fairy tales, though. At least as tall as a house.'

'Or even taller,' said Hasan. 'I've seen pictures of giants as tall as office-blocks.'

'The mistake about our size came about because people once took us for something else,' said the Giant. 'Many centuries ago, before people knew about dinosaurs they were puzzled by the huge bones they were constantly digging up. Because they knew countless legends and myths about giants they decided that the bones must be ours. And why not? At least they had heard about us. The bones were proof that we were indeed monstrously tall. Does that answer your question?'

'You mean people actually thought dinosaur bones were giants' bones?' asked Hasan in disbelief.

The Giant nodded.

Rani was satisfied with the explanation of the Giant's less than fairy-tale size, but Hasan wasn't. He went off to search the library shelves for books on dinosaurs.

What he found was something quite different, but equally fascinating.

It was a rather strange ghost story ...

THE MAN WHO BORED PEOPLE
TO DEATH

ANDREW COFFREY WAS AN INSENSITIVE BORE. HE WOULD
tell the same story over and over again, and whatever he said
would always somehow or other end up being about himself.
There was hardly a sentence he spoke without an 'I' in it, or a
'me' or a 'mine'. He was totally – but totally – insensitive to
other people's feelings. If someone said to him, 'I've just suf-
fered a tragic loss,' he would reply, 'Oh yes, but can you guess
what happened to me today?' Then off he would go.

One evening he was riding home on his horse when to his
surprise he found himself lost. This baffled him, for he took
the same path day after day, and even if he had been asleep his

horse would have known the way. The darker it grew the more hopeless his situation became, and he was relieved when he saw a small cottage outlined on the horizon just ahead of him.

He tethered his horse to a tree, and after knocking and receiving no reply, he pushed open the cottage door and peered inside. The single-roomed cottage was uninhabited, even though a fire blazed away in the grate. Beside the fire was a chair into which he sat himself down, all the while wondering why there was no one about.

It was then he heard the voice.

'Andrew Coffrey, Andrew Coffrey!' it called.

He looked everywhere, inside and out, but as there was not a soul to be seen he returned to the chair beside the fire.

'Andrew Coffrey, Andrew Coffrey, tell me a story!'

The voice was louder than before, and Andrew Coffrey thought someone must be playing a trick on him. He was beginning to grow angry when suddenly from a cupboard in the corner of the room stepped a man. It wasn't so much seeing a man step out the cupboard that shocked him, it was seeing who the man was. It was a man called Patrick Rooney whom everyone knew Coffrey had literally bored to death many years ago.

The corpse of Patrick Rooney stood swaying beside the

cupboard door, repeating over and over again, 'Andrew Coffrey, Andrew Coffrey, tell me a story, or it'll be the worse for you!'

As much as he loved telling a good story, Andrew Coffrey was out the cottage in a flash and didn't rest till he was safely hidden up a tree a mile or so away. He had hardly got his breath back when he heard a rustling of leaves and saw four men approaching the tree carrying an open coffin between them. Inside it lay the corpse of Patrick Rooney. They dumped it down beneath the tree then carried on their way, unaware of anyone above them.

After about an hour Andrew Coffrey decided it must be safe to get down again, for Patrick Rooney hadn't moved an inch and looked as dead as ever. But the moment Coffrey's feet touched the ground up sat the body, eyes glittering and teeth razor-sharp.

'Andrew Coffrey, Andrew Coffrey, tell me a story, or it'll be the worse for you!'

Andrew Coffrey didn't stop to enquire what the worse might be, but rushed off into the night in a state of panic. Without knowing exactly how it happened, he found himself back in the cottage, once again sitting in the chair beside the fire. A moment later the corpse came stumbling in after him.

'Andrew Coffrey, Andrew Coffrey, tell me a story,' it said.

By now Andrew Coffrey was absolutely exhausted. He was fed up with hearing the same thing over and over again, and his fear turned to anger.

'The strangest story I know is the one that's happening to me right now,' he said, 'and it's the only story you'll get out of me, for it's the best there is!'

'It is exactly the one I want to hear,' said the corpse.

And so with the corpse standing right there in front of him, Andrew Coffrey told the story of how he got lost and of how he found the cottage and of how he came inside and of how he sat in the chair and of how he saw the corpse and of how he climbed the tree and of how he then climbed out the tree, and so on and so on, and when he was finished the corpse said to him, 'Andrew Coffrey, Andrew Coffrey, tell me the story again.'

The corpse wouldn't let him go. It held him with a supernatural power and every time he finished the story, the corpse demanded to hear it again.

'Aren't you bored with it yet?' Coffrey asked after the thirty-seventh re-telling, and Patrick Rooney's ghost replied, 'Andrew Coffrey, Andrew Coffrey, tell it again.'

Andrew Coffrey repeated the story till he thought he must go mad. His tongue ached, his throat was parched and his lips were numb. He promised himself that if ever he escaped the demon's clutches he would never, but *never*, repeat any story that had anything to do with himself ever again.

It could have been his promise never to tell another story about himself, or simply the heat from the fire, but whatever it was Andrew Coffrey found himself falling asleep in mid-sentence.

When he woke he was once again sitting on his horse riding home.

'What a peculiar thing to have happened to me,' he said to himself.

A little while later, forgetting his promise, he thought how wonderful it would be to recount his strange adventure to the people back home. Why, it was so interesting that he was sure he could tell the story over and over again without people getting bored.

He was thinking this thought when, to his surprise, he found himself lost. This baffled him, for he took the same path day after day, and even if he had been asleep his horse would have known the way. The darker it grew the more hopeless his situation became, and he was relieved when he saw a small cottage outlined on the horizon just ahead of him ...

—⁓—

If the Story Giant had needed any confirmation other than his own pain that – unless his story was found – he was indeed living through his last night, it came while Hasan was busy reading the ghost story. The Giant suddenly realized that the stones of the Castle had begun to react to his illness. The rafters creaked and groaned, and in distant, half-forgotten corridors, tiny fragments of stone tumbled, almost inaudibly, to the ground. The Castle was now mirroring his own decay, and it ached along with his bones.

He was brought back to himself by Bett's voice, as she began telling her first story. She had decided that as they would all be telling stories for a while yet, she'd show them how it was done. The story was one a Japanese Buddhist friend of her mother's had told her. She stood in the centre of the library, acting out the story as much as telling it, mimicking the different voices, pausing for effect, sometimes whispering, sometimes speeding up the words. Her face registered surprise, shock, fear. She used her whole body in the telling. She was brilliant.

THE SPIRIT-FOXES

THERE WAS A VILLAGE IN JAPAN WHERE EVERYONE BELIEVED foxes were magical beings, inside which lived spirits that delighted in tricking people. The one exception was a man called Tokutaro, a nasty piece of work who took every opportunity to ridicule his neighbours' beliefs.

'Even if spirits did inhabit foxes, they would never fool me,' he boasted.

Eventually his companions grew sick of his sneering and challenged him.

'If you stay overnight in the fields where the spirit-foxes live, and if nothing happens to you, we'll provide you with all the wine and food you need for a year,' they said. 'But if something does happen to you and the foxes trick you, then it is us you'll have to pay.'

Tokutaro accepted the challenge.

'I'm going to have the most wonderful year,' he said, and immediately set off to win his bet.

By dusk Tokutaro had arrived at a place where a grove of bamboo shivered and whispered in the wind. He watched as a fox entered the grove, and soon afterwards saw a young girl walking out just ahead of him. Could the villagers have been right after all? he wondered. His suspicions aroused, Tokutaro followed behind the girl, vainly searching for a fox's tail. In time she came to a small wooden house that squatted in a yard littered with the skeletons of chickens and other small creatures that foxes found tasty. It was the bones more than anything that convinced Tokutaro it really was a spirit-fox he had been following.

Tokutaro waited for her to leave, but at last impatience got the better of him and he burst into the house where he found the girl and her parents crouching beside a smoking fire.

When he told her startled parents their daughter was really a fox in disguise, they tried to force him back outside. But they were no match for Tokutaro, who pushed them away and with a brutal blow knocked the girl to the ground.

'Change back into your true shape!' he screamed, stamping

on the girl and kicking her as hard as he could. Such was his rage that he eventually killed the girl, and still there was no transformation.

Her grief-stricken parents finally managed to overcome Tokutaro. They tied him to a chair, and were wondering whether to kill him themselves or take him down to the village to be hanged, when a wandering priest appeared at the door and begged the old couple to spare him.

'No doubt he has been bewitched by the spirit-foxes,' said the priest. 'It happens that I need a disciple. If he agrees to have his head shaved and his face tattooed with the mask of a fox in penance for his terrible deed, then I will take him.'

Much to Tokutaro's amazement the girl's parents agreed to this strange suggestion. And Tokutaro himself was more than happy to agree. It was a small price to pay for not being murdered by the grieving parents, or hanged by the village court.

The dead girl's parents brought a razor and needles. Tokutaro's head was shaved, and his face was painfully tattooed with indelible ink.

The moment the last pin-prick had entered his cheek there was a clap of thunder and loud peals of laughter shook the little wooden house.

It crumbled around him, turned to dust, and vanished.

Tokutaro found himself sitting alone in the fields. The

body of the girl had vanished. Her parents and the priest had vanished. He looked for them, but all he saw were four foxes dancing with glee out on the horizon.

Tokutaro's head was bald. On his face was tattooed the hideous mask of a grinning fox. He had lost his bet.

—〰—

'He must have felt like shooting a few foxes after that experience,' said Hasan. 'Do you still do that in Britain, Liam? Play hunt-the-fox? It is something my father did once. He wore a red coat and tally-hoed all over the place. Why do you wear red coats to hunt the foxes, Liam?'

Liam did not respond to Hasan's taunt. He'd taken a book – *Tarka the Otter* – from a shelf and was sitting hunched up in his duffel coat studying the illustrations. Realizing that his attention-seeking was having no effect on Liam, Hasan tried a different tack. He asked the Giant a question he knew he would get an answer to.

'All the hundreds and hundreds of stories here,' he said, waving his hand around the library, 'did any of them really happen, are any of them really real?'

'If you believe in something enough, then on one level or another it must exist,' said the Giant.

'Not necessarily,' replied Hasan, 'it is still only imagining. I can believe in something without it existing.'

'Perhaps, but belief is a very powerful thing. If I said someone who was freezing to death could survive simply by blowing on glow-worms, what would you say?'

'I'd say it was impossible.'

'Even if I explained how it was done?'

'It can't be done.'

'Oh, yes it can,' said the Story Giant. 'Listen.'

HOPE

'ONE BITTERLY COLD NIGHT,' SAID THE STORY GIANT, 'a band of monkeys agreed they would freeze to death unless they imitated a group of humans they had seen huddled around a camp-fire. They had no idea how to make fire. All they knew was that it seemed to keep the human beings warm.

'One monkey said it thought it knew where the humans got their fire from, and it sent the rest out searching for fire-flies and glow-worms. They gathered as many as they could and covered them with twigs and dry leaves. Then they all sat round blowing gently on the glow-worms in the hope of producing flames.

'A monkey who thought itself superior to the rest sat at a distance from them, shivering and mocking their efforts.

'"That's not how humans make fire," it taunted between shivers. "You can blow for eternity, but it'll never work."

'The other monkeys ignored the taunts. They kept blowing on the dry leaves, concentrating on how lovely and warm they would be once the fire caught. The monkey who imagined itself superior carried on taunting them, but as the night grew colder and colder its taunts were heard less and less.

'At dawn the others found it curled up in a crevice between two rocks, its mouth and beard rimmed with ice. It had frozen to death. Its companions had not succeeded in making fire, but they had survived because they'd had the one thing the dead monkey did not have, and it had kept them alive.'

'And what was that thing?' asked Hasan.

'It was Hope,' said the Giant, 'and the belief that they might actually succeed in creating fire.'

'But they still didn't manage to light a fire, did they?'

The Giant sighed. 'You're being pedantic, Hasan, and you know it. Believing they could create fire helped them to survive the cold. It was only the cynical monkey who froze to death. The one without hope.

Imagine an athlete running in the Olympics. If he was totally convinced he was going to lose the race, if he had no belief or hope, do you think he would stand even the remotest chance of winning?'

Hasan knew that the Giant was right. One of Hasan's problems was that he needed to hear things many times over before he believed them. If he were told blue and yellow made green, he would ask, 'Why?' and he would not be content until he'd had the reason explained in as many different ways as possible. He knew it was a fault of his that irritated everyone. He would take nothing at face value.

'You're enough to make even Djuha despair' was a favourite expression of his father's. Hasan had liked that.

Djuha was a character known all over the Arab world who believed for every question asked there were at least thousand possible replies.

He was loved for his mixture of humour and wisdom, and at home Hasan had endless comics full of Djuha's adventures, just as his father had books that explained the wisdom behind the Djuha stories.

Remembering the stories excited Hasan. There were so many of them that he imagined there must be at least one amongst them that the Giant did not know. He leapt up from where he'd been sitting beside Petra and told the first Djuha story that came into his head.

THE CLOTHES THAT WERE
INVITED TO DINNER

A WEALTHY MAN WHO WAS ALSO A TERRIBLE SNOB WAS
giving a huge dinner party with fantastic food prepared by
his personal chef. The man liked having famous and interesting people at his dinners and though he had never met
him, he invited a man called Djuha who was known for his
wisdom.

Djuha wasn't interested in worldly things and when he
came along dressed in his usual grubby old clothes he was
turned away for looking like a tramp.

Djuha returned home and dug out the one good set of
clothes he owned from the back of the wardrobe. He returned

to the party, and this time because he was well dressed he was allowed in.

The first course was chicken soup, which Djuha promptly poured over his coat. The next course was fish. Djuha raised his arm, took the fish, and dropped it down his sleeve.

The dinner guests tried their best to ignore his strange behaviour, but when he started squashing strawberries into the turn-ups of his trousers, they decided they'd had enough.

'What on earth are you doing, fool?'

'I'm feeding my clothes,' said Djuha, 'for after all, it was they who were invited to this dinner party, not me.'

—⁓—

When Hasan finished the story, the Giant burst out laughing. 'Well done, Hasan! The Djuha stories are as good as medicine to me!'

'Do you know them *all*?' asked Hasan.

The look of disappointment on Hasan's face when the Giant nodded yes was witnessed by everyone. Hasan was desperate for the Giant to find his missing story, no matter who told it, but he would have loved it to have been him.

'In some countries Djuha is known as a rascal called Ben Sikran and in other countries as a teacher called Nasrudin or Hodja,' said the Story

Giant. ' It is believed that when one Djuha story is told, it is impossible for another not to come rushing after it.'

'Then tell us another,' said Betts. 'They sound neat.'

Hasan wasn't sure whether Betts was talking to him or to the Giant, but whichever, another story leapt to his tongue immediately.

A SIMPLE TRICK

Dᴊᴜʜᴀ sᴏᴍᴇᴛɪᴍᴇs ᴡᴏʀᴋᴇᴅ ᴀs ᴀ ᴛᴇᴀᴄʜᴇʀ ᴀɴᴅ ᴏɴᴇ ᴅᴀʏ ʜᴇ overheard one of his students boasting that nobody could trick him.

'I'm sure I could find a way,' said Djuha. 'Wait here a moment and when I return I'm sure I'll have thought of a fool-proof way to trick you.'

A couple of hours later Djuha's student was still waiting for him to return when another student passed by.

'Have you seen Djuha?' asked the first student, who was growing more and more irritated waiting for his teacher.

'He's just gone off on his holidays,' said the second student, 'but before he left he gave me a message for you. He said you can stop waiting for him the moment you realize how easily you can be tricked.'

—⁓—

The Story Giant obviously loved the Djuha stories, because as soon as Hasan had finished telling the second story, the Giant himself began on a third.

DEGREES OF SORROW
AND HAPPINESS

WHEN A MAN LOST HIS DONKEY EVERYONE DECIDED TO HELP him look for it. One of the people who joined in the search was Djuha, whom many people thought a fool, but who was in fact an extremely wise man.

Djuha searched for the missing donkey as thoroughly as everyone else, but while they went about with long faces shaking their heads and sighing about how awful it was to lose a donkey, Djuha went about his task singing.

'It's terrible to be singing when someone's lost his donkey,' they berated him.

'I'm not singing because the man has lost his donkey,' said

Djuha, 'for that makes me sad. I am singing because it is not mine, and that makes me happy.'

—ɯ—

'How many Djuha stories are there?' Betts asked the Story Giant. 'What do you think, Hasan? Hundreds?'

'Thousands,' said Hasan.

'Maybe not thousands,' said the Giant. 'Sometimes stories get attached to characters when really they are from elsewhere. Do you know the story of the shadow in the desert, Hasan?'

Hasan shook his head. 'No.'

'It is more than two thousand years old,' said the Giant. 'I first heard it while sitting in a tent on the edge of the Sahara Desert. It could easily be mistaken for a Djuha story.'

THE SHADOW

ONE MORNING A RICH MAN HIRED A DRIVER AND HIS CAMEL to cross a desert to the town where he lived. By late afternoon the sun's heat was overpowering. Ordering the driver to stop, the rich man sat down in the camel's shadow. The driver, who was the stronger of the two men, pushed him aside and sat in the shadow himself.

'I've paid you for the hire of this animal,' complained the rich man.

'True,' said the driver, 'but you did not pay me for the hire of its shadow.'

Hasan was itching to tell a final Djuha story, but while he was wondering which one to tell, Rani was beginning a story of her own. 'It is about an Angel,' she said. 'And about the Mother of the prophet Jesus.'

A HANDFUL OF CORN

A WOMAN CALLED MARY WAS FLEEING TO EGYPT WITH HER son. She had enemies who wished to kill the boy, and she was afraid for him.

An Angel appeared at the roadside and as Mary came by, he gave her a bag of corn. 'Hand this on to the first people you meet and tell them to plant it immediately,' he said.

Hardly a moment had passed when Mary saw two men harvesting a field of ripe wheat. She told them what the Angel had asked her to do, and they took the corn and planted it among the full-grown wheat. The next day Mary's enemies came to the field and asked the men if they had seen a woman carrying a child. They said they had, for they'd been forbidden by Mary to lie.

'How long ago did you see them?' asked the hunters.

'On the day we planted the new corn,' they replied.

Mary's enemies looked at the field of fully grown wheat and decided for themselves she must have passed long ago. They turned back the way they'd come, thinking by now she must be so far ahead of them that it would be useless pursuing her any longer.

—ɯ—

Hasan, still determined to tell a final Djuha story, chose one of the shortest he could remember. Unfortunately for him, it was also one of the most baffling, and one he had never really understood.

THE LAMP

ONE DAY DJUHA BOASTED THAT HE COULD SEE IN THE DARK.

'Rubbish, whenever you go out at night you always carry a lamp,' said his neighbour.

'Of course I do,' said Djuha. 'That is why I can see in the dark.'

'Very amusing,' replied Djuha's neighbour. 'If you are so clever, I'm sure you will be able to tell me why the flame from your lamp gives off light.'

'Certainly,' said Djuha, 'but first of all you must tell me where the light goes when I blow out the flame.'

Liam was getting bored with the Djuha stories. After Hasan's very short tale he decided they were all about to disintegrate into jokes, and so he'd switched off. He shrank into his duffel coat like a fox into its den. He doubted the story the Giant needed to find would be anything as brief as the one Hasan had just told. It had to be darker and more mysterious, he decided. Lost in these thoughts, he missed the next story to be told.

THE PLACE AHEAD

A WISE MAN WAS SITTING RESTING AT A CROSSROADS SITUATED at an equal distance between two towns when a traveller approached him and asked, 'What is it like in the town up ahead?'

'What was it like in the town you've just come from?' asked the wise man.

'It was an awful place,' the traveller said. 'The people were mean and unfriendly. They were absolutely stupid. I couldn't get on with them at all.'

'I'm afraid you'll find the town up ahead just the same,' said the wise man.

A short time later another traveller approached the crossroads. He had come from the same town as the first traveller and he too wanted to know what it was like in the town up ahead.

'Tell me about the town from which you have just come,' the wise man asked again. 'What was it like?'

'It was a wonderful place,' said the second traveller. 'I couldn't have hoped to meet friendlier people. They were a joy to be with.'

'Then I am sure you will find the town up ahead exactly the same,' the wise man replied.

Really, Liam's irritation with the stories had little to do with Hasan, and far more to do with being cooped up. He had begun to feel trapped in the library.

The heat from the fire had caused him to feel drowsy and, as the murmur of voices around him grew more and more muted, he felt himself drifting from the room. It was like a sleep within a sleep. Soon he was walking along one of the Castle's innumerable corridors and out into a courtyard surrounded by tall, ivy-clad walls. He stretched out on an ancient stone bench in the centre of the courtyard and looked up at the stars.

He felt comfortable again now that he was outside. He was aware that the sounds he could hear were the same noises he heard night after night from the bunk of the boat he lived on with his father. In fact, part of his dreaming self knew they were the same noises and that he was really on the boat, asleep.

He listened to the screech-owls and barking fox-cubs and wondered whether the Giant's missing story would ever be found – he was certain that he, Liam, could not help. It bothered him that he seemed to know so few stories. Or rather, that they were locked away inside him.

Just then a shadow fell across him. He looked up, straight into the face of Betts who was standing beside the bench, watching him. He sat up and made room for her.

'I saw you leave,' she said, sitting down beside him. 'Do you think he will ever find his story?'

'The Giant?' Liam shrugged. He didn't really know what to say. After a pause, he added: 'I thought you told the story about the foxes brilliantly.'

'Really? It's a talent I inherited from my mother. She was in films. But then everyone in LA is in films.'

'LA?'

'Los Angeles. It's where I come from. In America. What about you?'

'I live near here, on the river with Dad. Mum lives in Australia. They're divorced now, but they're still friends.'

'Why Australia?'

'It's where she's from. Dad met her when he was a student, travelling over there. It's where I was born. We all came back together, but Mum got homesick. I was in school by then, and had some good mates. So I stayed on with Dad.'

'Do you miss it?'

'Australia? Sometimes. We lived in the outback. I loved the animals there. Have you got tiger-cats in America, or wombats?'

'Animals aren't my scene. How come you like them so much?'

'They're magic. Was she successful?' Liam deflected the conversation away from himself.

'Eh? Excuse me?'

'Your mum. Was she a successful actress?'

'What do you think? We live in two rooms above an all-night super-market. It's not exactly the kind of place where you'd find your regular movie-star. Anyway, I want to act for real. The stage. You know any plays?'

Liam shook his head. 'What does she do now?' he asked.

'Don't ask. OK, do. She drinks. You name it, she drinks it. She's a star at drinking.'

Liam felt his chance to impress Betts slipping away. She talked and thought too fast for him. All he could think to do was repeat his opening remark, as if that could set the conversation in motion again. 'You did, you told the story brilliantly.'

He could smell the scent of sleep drifting from her and evaporating in the cold night air. He thought how strange it was that they were dreaming the same dream but he still could not speak to her the way he wanted to.

After a moment, Betts said, 'I'm going back in. How about you? Isn't it time you told a story or two?'

Liam didn't answer, and eventually she shrugged and went back in.

When she'd gone he huddled inside his duffel coat and stretched back down on the bench. He could see the Milky Way and Orion above him. The sky was exactly the way he saw it through the port-hole beside his bunk-bed.

Walking back from the courtyard to the library Betts was thinking about the Giant. She knew in his situation she would be panicking, rushing from shelf to shelf and tearing open books in search of the missing story, but it was obviously not in the Giant's nature to panic. Whatever turmoil the Story Giant was feeling he kept locked inside him. She was half-way down the corridor when she remembered another of the stories her mother's Japanese friend had told. It could have been Liam praising the way she had told her first story that made her remember it, or maybe it was simply because the corridor was spooky, and the story had contained a monster of kinds. Whichever, she told the story the moment she arrived back in the library.

THE MONSTER IN THE DESERT

A GROUP OF TRAVELLERS ARRIVED IN A TOWN ON THE EDGE of a desert where the soil was like grey dust, and nothing grew except for a few twisted thorn trees. The townspeople were as hospitable as it was possible to be in such circumstances. They provided the travellers with just enough water to cross the desert safely, warning them that in the desert itself there was not a single drop to be found. They also warned the travellers about an extraordinary monster that lived in the desert. They said it delighted in tricking and killing people. Not since Time began, they said, had there been a more cunning or devious monster. They warned the travellers to be on their guard day and night.

All went well at first. The leader of the camel-train measured out the exact amount of water each person needed. He kept four guards in front of the camel-train and four guards behind it, and he ordered everyone to report the slightest suspicious thing they saw.

There were the usual petty squabbles and fights among the travellers but nothing serious occurred, and it was only when they were nearing the centre of the desert and the heat grew intolerable that they began to complain. They had also begun to think that since they'd gone for days without seeing the slightest living thing, perhaps the townspeople had been wrong about there being a monster in the desert. They were fed up having to be so vigilant. It made them irritable. And the more irritable they became, the more argumentative and inattentive they grew.

On the day they arrived at the centre of the desert they met another camel-train coming from the opposite direction. But unlike them, these people were happy and relaxed. What's more, they had such an abundance of water it sloshed about everywhere. When asked about the monster they said that they had not even known one was supposed to exist.

'The only thing we've seen in the desert is the well,' they said.

'A well?'

'We passed it a little while back. It's surrounded by trees and lush green grass, and its water is sweet and clear.'

This was fantastic news. Neither camel-train had seen a monster and there was an abundance of water! A party was soon underway. People from both camel-trains sat up late into the night singing and guzzling all the water they wanted, and splashing it about everywhere. Then they all snuggled down to sleep contentedly under the stars.

At dawn the people from the first camel-train woke to find themselves alone. There was no sign of the second camel-train. It seemed to have evaporated into the night. And as the blazing sun rose above the horizon, they saw there were no footprints or hoof-marks in front of them, and that behind them were only their own tracks. With mounting horror they realized that the second camel-train had been an illusion – it had been the monster in disguise.

The townspeople's warning echoed through their minds: *'Not since Time began has there been such a cunning or devious monster.'*

They had met it, and it had tricked them. Their water had been squandered, and ahead of them, the burning, waterless desert waited to consume them all.

—⁓—

Betts had finished her story by the time Liam returned from the courtyard. When he entered the library she was standing with Rani, peering out of the window on the far side of the room. Rani was worried that there might be dragons prowling around. 'In fairy-tales, you *always* find them outside castles,' she was saying.

It was this absurd worry of Rani's that finally enabled Liam to tell a story: he reckoned if he made dragons sound silly, then she wouldn't fear them. And in telling a story, he also helped himself. It was as if a door had suddenly opened inside his head, or a stone had been rolled away from the entrance to a cave in which his imagination had been trapped. (Of course, Liam being Liam, he mumbled his story, and Hasan kept interrupting him and telling him to speak more clearly. Liam could have murdered him, showing him up in front of Betts like that.)

THE DRAGON SLAYER'S MUM

An old lady once killed a dragon with a pudding. In legends it's usually heroes who kill dragons. You know the kind of thing: a knight in flashy armour comes and slays a fire-breathing dragon as big as a double-decker bus with one thrust of his mighty sword. Well, if you're going to believe that kind of thing, more fool you. An old lady killing a dragon with a pudding might not be quite as romantic, but it's a bit more realistic.

The old dear's name was Meg Puttock and though her son usually gets all the credit for killing the dragon, it was really her who managed it.

Meg lived in the north of England near a marshy lake called Knucker Hole and below the lake lived the dragon.

The lake was called Knucker Hole because in Meg's day dragons were often called Knuckers.

It was a pretty lucky dragon. It was discovered on the very day the world's number one dragon-slayer retired, and so there was no one around who could defeat it. It was therefore free to eat all the cows and people it fancied. The one thing it wasn't very fond of was sheep. The woolly bits kept getting stuck in its teeth.

One day Meg was outside her cottage feeding birds with the remains of an old pudding she'd cooked when the dragon came along and helped itself to a bit.

It decided that Meg's puddings were almost as tasty as people, and as it liked to vary its diet it told Meg it would spare her and her family if she cooked it some more puddings.

Now, Meg wasn't the world's greatest cook. Her puddings were stodgy and heavy and gave everyone indigestion, but they tasted heavenly to the dragon.

Meg made as many as she could and each pudding was stodgier and bigger than the last. The dragon ate so many it couldn't move, and lay burping and bloated in Meg's vegetable patch.

As soon as it fell asleep Meg took her frying pan, a big black one covered in bits of burnt food and grease, and bashed the dragon over the head with it. She broke its skull as if its skull were no thicker than a robin's egg. Her son George, who at the time was an apprentice butcher, cut the dragon up into manageable pieces and sold it off in the market-place while boasting to everyone that *he* had killed it.

People believed him, and he's famous right up to this very day. He's known all over the world as St George, the Dragon-Slayer. But it was really his mum, Meg, who killed the dragon with her puddings and her frying pan, not him.

Rani thought the story was hysterically funny and wanted another. 'OK,' Liam mumbled. 'Just one.'

But it would not be just one. Liam, the last to tell a story, had been firmly drawn in to the group now. The Castle's enchantment had finally worked its magic on him. He stood among the books in the Story Giant's library, and just as little bubbles rise from the bottom of a glass, so stories from his childhood rose unbidden from his memory.

He remembered how, as a young child in the outback his mother had told him stories that came from the original inhabitants of Australia, the Aborigines. All their stories were from a time they called Dreamtime, a time before people existed when the land was occupied by a race of semi-human giants, godlike creatures who were responsible for everything that later came into being. One of their stories was about a frog.

TIDDALIK THE FROG

ONCE THERE WAS A FROG CALLED TIDDALIK. HE WAS THE largest frog that had ever existed, as big as a dinosaur only much fatter. He was also the gloomiest frog there had ever been. Tiddalik spent his time beneath mountain-sized boulders and wore a perpetual frown on his big green face. One day he developed an incredible thirst and began to drink an entire lake dry. This didn't quench his thirst, so he moved to a river and he drank that dry as well. There seemed no end to the amount of water he needed and he moved from place to place, drinking and drinking and drinking. Soon he had drunk every drop of water in the entire land.

The grass shrivelled, the trees died and the soil turned to

dust. The other creatures feared for their lives and would no doubt have died had not a wise old wombat come up with the solution to the Tiddalik problem.

'We must make the miserable old thing laugh,' he said. "Then the muscles in its belly will contract and all the water will flow out again.'

So the animals tried to make the frog laugh. First the kangaroo tried dancing about on her tail juggling with baby koala bears, but this didn't get a response. Then a duck-billed platypus told a confusing joke that no one understood.

Everyone had a go. The dingo and the kiwi, the bush-baby and the ostrich, the crocodile and the cockatoo all took a turn at trying to amuse the unamused frog, but it was no use. The great gloomy frog sat under his mountain-sized boulder wearing a great gloomy frown and the world grew more and more barren.

It was only when Nabunum the eel began tying himself in knots that things changed. A glimmer appeared in Tiddalik's eye, and when the eel attempted a belly-dance the frog roared with laughter. Sure enough, just as the wise old wombat had predicted, all the water the frog had drunk flowed back out of his mouth, and the lakes and rivers came back again.

—ɯ—

W hen he finished the Tiddalik story, Liam said to the Giant, 'You know that story as well, don't you? It's come from the opposite side of the planet but you know it.'

The Giant nodded almost imperceptibly.

It was that tiny nod of the head that made Liam realize how much the Giant longed to hear the story he did not know, and Liam felt he understood a little more about the Giant's nature. Exactly how much pain and grief he was hiding away from them all hardly bore thinking of.

There was a smell about the Giant, a faint muskiness that rose from him and hung in the air around him, a haunted scent that only Liam with his natural affinity for the animal world was aware of. It was fox-like, but nowhere near as sharp or pungent. And Liam imagined how the Story Giant must had lived like a fox among humankind, hiding, and forever on guard. He felt privileged that the Giant had woven him into his secret world.

The children sat around in the library and story after story went back and forth. Tales they thought they had forgotten came back to them, and under the Giant's influence they found themselves changing and adding to them, helping the stories to evolve as the Giant had forecast. But if any contained a clue as to the plot of the missing story then the children were unaware of it.

And the Castle listened along with them, its walls soaking up their tales with a stony impatience, as if it, too, were longing to hear the one story that evaded them all.

The Giant could tell that there had been an acceleration in the Castle's disintegration, but he tried not to show his anxiety. As his weariness grew, so the building continued to unravel. It was not so noticeable in the library, where his influence was still strongest, but in unvisited attics on the outer edges of the Castle, manuscripts safely stored away for centuries were decaying and turning to dust. Mildew was spreading through the rooms, infinitesimal cracks were widening, and the voices of the stories embedded inside the walls whispered and murmured in confusion. In the courtyard the bench on which Liam had stretched himself out had collapsed, and lunar moths that had sought refuge among the ivy fluttered off in search of a less disturbing home.

The night was passing and the longed-for story was as big a mystery as ever.

Occasionally the Giant reminisced about the past, telling the children of the wonderful things he had seen on his journeys through the ancient world. He told stories in such a way that the children could not tell whether or not what he was saying was true. Of course to him it did not matter, for to the Giant all stories were true: 'truth' and 'stories' were one and the same thing, and if the children asked, 'Is that true?' he would reply, 'Whose truth do you mean? The truth of the story-teller who can make anything happen, or the truth of someone who is endlessly asking for proof?'

Once when Hasan, who had been thinking about the fantastic length of time the Giant had lived, asked him what it had been like before money was invented, the Giant had replied that he'd once visited a country where colour was used as a currency.

'Blue, green, jade, red, amber, purple, orange, mauve and pink – each colour could buy different things,' said the Story Giant. 'Food, for example, could be bought with the colour green. A green cube or piece of green cloth would buy you anything that grew from the earth or was edible. And because the ocean and sky were blue, then blue was the colour you used if you wished to travel. If you wished to stay overnight at an inn, then grey was the colour you used, because grey was the colour of the dusk, and dusk was when people settled down for the night.'

The Giant said he thought this had been a wonderful use of colour, but that the practice had passed into history because people began to value one colour above another. Hasan thought the story absurd, but really it was no more fanciful than many of the stories he had accepted without comment.

One story Rani objected to – not because it was weird but simply because she thought it was gruesome – had been told by the Giant in the form of a poem. He'd sat back in his chair, half-reciting and half-singing the story of an owl who'd found a perfect way to preserve its food.

THE OWL'S TRICK

From its hollow and ancient tree
An owl looked down and said to me,
'About my feet are swarms of mice
And I can easily leave them there,
For from their feet I've ripped their toes
And now they'll not go anywhere.
I eat them slowly at my ease,
I pick and choose them as I please.
The fattest ones I let digest
Before indulging in the rest.
I bring them corn into my croft,
It keeps them living, fresh, and soft.
Before this trick occurred to me
They were nimble and scurried free.
I've neatly torn the paws from each
Panicking creature in my reach.
My larder's stocked throughout the night,
And there's no need for endless flight.'

'That's horrible,' said Rani, who halfway through the poem had covered her ears with her hands. 'Why do things have to be so horrid? It is cruel.'

'If you drown a mouse in honey, is it any less cruel than drowning it in salt water?' asked the Giant.

Rani had no reply to that. She put her hands firmly in her lap and stared at the Giant defiantly. 'I like nice animals,' she declared.

The Story Giant understood the contradictions in Rani's nature. Even though some of the stories she told contained cruelty, she wished that the world were a better place than she instinctively knew it to be.

'The Owl is an Æsop story, isn't it?' asked Liam. 'I was given a book of them once. They sounded school-teachery.'

'Don't blame old Æsop for that,' said the Giant. 'It's the way they've been translated and handed down over the centuries that's the problem. *He* thought their meanings were clear enough without the need for morals tagged to the end of them. It was later generations that went to such great lengths to do that – as if people couldn't work the stories out for themselves. Anyway, most were no more written by Æsop than Grimm's Fairy Tales were written by the Grimm brothers. He simply gathered them and tossed in a few of his own. Æesop was a slave, you know.'

'A slave?' asked Betts. 'Did you know him?'

'I was living in what is now Afghanistan when he was around. By the time I got to Greece where he was supposed to have been living he had vanished. Rumour had it he'd been flung over a cliff at Delphi.'

'One of my distant relatives was a slave,' said Betts. 'A long, long time ago.'

Liam looked at her, incredulous.

'She was African,' explained Betts. 'Half her village was captured by an enemy tribe and sold on to slave-traders. She was among thousands of people who were shipped from Africa to America to work on the cotton plantations.'

'But you don't look African,' said Liam.

'No more than millions who can trace their ancestry back to Africa do. Look at me carefully, Liam. What do you see?'

Liam was tongue-tied again.

'My great grandmother married into a family from Ecuador. Her daughter married a Spaniard from Argentina. My mother married a Texan who took her to California and dumped her. I suppose that makes me a pure-blooded American.'

'We have servants, not slaves,' said Hasan, sniffily.

Betts ignored him. 'Before the American Civil War the African slaves were forbidden to learn how to read or write, so all their stories were passed down the generations by word of mouth. Gran's favourites were the Brer Rabbit stories which she knew from her youth.'

'Why a rabbit?' asked Hasan. He felt he'd said something inappropriate about servants and slaves, but wasn't sure what.

'Because rabbits had to be crafty or they got eaten,' said Betts. 'And Brer meant brother, or friend. Not that Brer Rabbit had many friends. Half the world wanted to eat him. Survival was hard.'

BRER RABBIT AND
BRER ALLIGATOR

ONE DAY BRER RABBIT WAS BEING CHASED BY A DOG AND THE
only place he could find to hide was down by the creek where
Brer Alligator lived. He was hiding there, puffing and pant-
ing away, when Brer Alligator spotted him and asked,
'What's the problem, Brer Rabbit?'

'I'm hiding away from trouble,' said Brer Rabbit. 'I'm sick
of being chased all day.'

Now the alligator's brain was as small as his tail was long,
and when Brer Rabbit said he was hiding away from trouble
the alligator thought he was talking about a creature called
Trouble.

'I've been living down here all these years and I've never once met Brer Trouble. Any notion what he tastes like?'

Brer Rabbit understood immediately that Brer Alligator had got the wrong end of the stick, for the alligator had certainly eaten enough dogs in his time. 'Brer Trouble's hot and spicy, I guess,' said Brer Rabbit, hardly able to keep himself from smirking.

'Well now, I must confess I'm a mite fed up with eating rabbits. Nothing against you personally, Brer Rabbit, but after a while us alligators get a craving for something a bit tastier. Just now, something sharp and hot would suit me fine. What's this Brer Trouble look like?'

'Oh, trouble is *really* hard to describe,' he said. 'One day he's one thing, the next he's another.'

'You mean you can never recognize him, ever?' said Brer Alligator.

'Oh, most folk can recognize trouble after their first meeting,' said Brer Rabbit.

'Then you must arrange for us to meet – do that and I'll leave off chasing after you and all your babies for a good long while.'

'That's fine by me,' said Brer Rabbit. 'Let's meet here tomorrow morning and we'll both go looking for trouble.'

The next morning Brer Alligator was at the side of the creek waiting, but Brer Rabbit didn't show up. He'd been planning and scheming on how best to get his revenge on Brer Alligator for all the baby rabbits he'd eaten. He'd also hit on an idea to stop Brer Alligator wandering too far from the water.

Eventually, Brer Alligator grew impatient waiting for Brer Rabbit, so he decided to go and look for himself. 'Brer Trouble must be really shy and quiet,' thought Brer Alligator, 'hiding away from me all these years.' His vast stomach rumbled at the thought of a tasty new kind of meal.

Meanwhile Brer Rabbit was hiding up a tree waiting for Brer Alligator to pass under it.

As soon as he did, Brer Rabbit prised a wasp's nest from a fork in the tree and sent it crashing down on Brer Alligator's snout.

Brer Alligator was stung well and good, but on he went, still looking for Brer Trouble. Next, he passed a hill, and Brer Rabbit sneakily pushed a pile of stones down onto him. Brer Alligator was well and truly battered, but on he went, still looking for Brer Trouble.

When Brer Rabbit showed up on the path pretending he was simply late for their appointment, Brer Alligator told him about the wasps and the rocks. Brer Rabbit looked sympathetic and said he was sorry that Brer Alligator had been having a lot of trouble.

'Haven't had even one bite of him yet, but I'm sure looking

forward to meeting him,' said Brer Alligator, who was getting hungrier and hungrier by the minute. 'Just tell me where he is and I'll do the rest.'

And so Brer Rabbit directed Brer Alligator into a vast patch of dry broom-grass and told him that if he waited there long enough, trouble was sure to come looking for him. Next thing, Brer Rabbit scampered off to the far side of the broom-grass and, lighting a fire, shouted back, 'Trouble's coming!'

When Brer Alligator saw the fire he was a little frightened, but he was so hungry he decided to hang on for a while. 'I can't see Brer Trouble anywhere,' he shouted through the spreading smoke.

'I can see trouble everywhere!' Brer Rabbit shouted back.

Soon the broom-grass was well and truly ablaze. Brer Alligator thrashed about wildly and was lucky to get out of the burning grass alive. Bruised, burnt, and smoked like a kipper, he scurried back to the creek and plopped sizzling into the water with a great sigh.

For days he lay hiding in the mud with just his snout sticking up out the water in case Brer Trouble was around. When he'd recovered enough he shouted up to Brer Rabbit, who he knew was hiding somewhere nearby, 'This is all your doing! You should have told me Brer Trouble's got it in for us alligators. If I ever get near you, Brer Rabbit, you're lunch!'

From that time on Brer Alligator and Brer Rabbit never saw eye to eye, which didn't bother Brer Rabbit too much because the alligator stopped wandering all over the land and mostly spent his time slinking around the creek, just in case Brer Trouble was somewhere around.

—◦◦◦—

'The Brer Rabbit stories are some of the most famous folk-tales to come out of Africa,' said the Story Giant, 'but there are others that are far stranger. Did you ever hear the story of the talking skull, Betts? That's another story from Africa.'

'I know a poem about a talking skull,' said Betts. 'We've used it in acting classes.'

'Well, the poem was originally a story,' said the Giant, 'and it's –'

He stopped suddenly, and sat there by the fire open-mouthed. The pain he had felt earlier flooded through him once more, wiping his mind blank of all else. It ebbed quickly, but for a moment all he could do was to sit stock-still while his brain, and indeed his very soul, reassembled themselves.

'How late is it?' he whispered at last, his face ashen.

There was no clock in the room. On any other night his question would have been of little importance. Only tonight did Time matter to the Giant. Liam crossed to the window and looked out across the moor.

The moon was still up high and he could tell by the configuration of the stars that dawn was still some hours away.

He turned back into the room. 'The morning's a good way off yet,' he said.

The Giant breathed more easily. He rested back in his chair and, hesitantly, told the story of the talking skull. As he spoke, the Castle continued to unravel, and the smell of decay and despair thickened in the darkened rooms.

THE TALKING SKULL

ONE MORNING WHILE HE WAS OUT STALKING A DEER A hunter tripped over a human skull hidden in the grass.

'Watch your step, fool!' it cried.

The hunter looked around, but saw nobody.

'I'm here at your feet,' said the skull.

The astonished hunter gingerly picked up the skull and examined it. For a skull to be imbued with such supernatural powers it must have met a very strange death, he reasoned.

'What killed you?' he asked.

'Talking killed me,' said the skull.

Now the hunter's tribe was ruled by a king who disliked the hunter intensely, and the hunter thought he could curry

[104]

favour with the king if he presented him with such a remark-able object. So he put the skull in his hunting-bag and hurried back to his village.

The next morning before presenting himself to the king he checked that his imagination had not been playing tricks on him. He took the skull out of his bag and asked again, 'What killed you?' and again the skull replied, 'Talking killed me.'

Satisfied, the hunter approached the King.

'I've a remarkable gift for you,' he said.

'A gift? *You?* What can you offer a king?'

'A skull that talks, sire,' said the hunter.

'A talking skull? What kind of fool do you take me for?'

'I swear it's true, sire,' said the hunter. With a flourish and a great show of pomp he held up the skull and asked, 'What killed you?'

But this time the skull remained silent.

'Do not ridicule me,' said the King. 'Do not say another word.'

But the hunter would not listen. Again and again he asked, 'What killed you?' But the skull spoke not a word.

By now half the tribe had gathered round the hunter and the King, and the King felt belittled standing there giving the time of day to such a fool, a man who spoke to a skull and would not shut up even when ordered to do so.

'You've insulted me enough!' he roared, and he commanded the hunter to be dragged off to the forest and executed.

The hunter was beheaded and his head was thrown into the grass along with the skull that had been his downfall. The head provided a banquet for the ants and was picked clean within days.

It was only then that the first skull spoke again.

'What killed you, friend?' it asked the new skull lying beside it.

'Talking killed me,' said the second skull.

A silence hung over the library when the Giant had finished his story, which he had told awkwardly, still suffering from the shock of the pain that had gripped him. His face was still ashen and the trembling of his hands was more pronounced. The children could not meet his eye, and the four of them sat gazing into the fire, lost for words.

It was Betts who broke the awkward silence. For the want of something better to say, she said, as casually as she could manage, 'I prefer the Brer Rabbit story to the skull story. I like the idea of something small and fluffy being so cunning. It's neat.'

'I know a story about cunning!' cried Rani, attempting to brighten the atmosphere. 'I shall tell it. And you will all be happy.' She spoke the last sentence as if it were an order, and the Giant smiled at her valiant effort to lift his spirits.

MAN IS CUNNING,
AND CUNNING IS MAN

ONCE WHEN THE WORLD WAS ALMOST BRAND NEW, DONKEY
went to Lion to complain about Man.

Lion, who had not yet seen Man and who didn't know
what he looked like, asked Donkey the exact nature of his
complaint.

'Well, Man puts heavy loads on my back and hits me to make
me go faster, even though he can't carry half the weight I can.'

Lion thought this was unfair and decided that Donkey was
hard done by.

'I'll sort this Man creature out for you,' he said. 'What does
he look like?'

'Well, for a start, he only has two legs instead of four. He can neither bray nor roar, and he hasn't got much fur.'

'How about scales? Has he got scales or any other distinguishing features?'

'None that I know of,' said Donkey. 'Though he does have hands.'

'Hands?'

'They're a bit like paws without claws,' said Donkey.

'Well, he shouldn't be too hard to find,' said Lion. And he set out to teach Man a lesson for being so cruel.

Soon Lion came across the first man he had ever seen. Now, Donkey's description had been pretty good, but Lion wanted to make sure he wasn't about to eat up the wrong creature. After all, birds only had two legs, and they couldn't bray or roar either.

'Are you Man?' asked Lion.

Fortunately the man was a bit of a trickster. 'No,' he said, 'I'm Cunning.'

'Well, it is Man I'm looking for, not Cunning. Why are you here?'

'I'm on my way to see Donkey. He's asked me to build a cage for him,' said Man.

This annoyed Lion. Remember, all this took place when the world was almost brand new, and Lion had no more idea what a cage was than what a man was. Still, he felt that being a lion, and therefore a more important animal than a donkey, he should have a cage first.

'If you want to see this day through, then you'd better forget Donkey,' threatened Lion. 'It is me you should be making a cage for.'

'I quite agree,' said Man. 'In my opinion it would suit you far better than it would suit Donkey.'

Man set about making the strongest cage he could, and when it was finished he invited Lion to step inside. Lion obliged, and Man slammed shut the cage door.

'Why are you doing this to me?' cried Lion. 'My enemy is Man, not Cunning.'

'Man *is* cunning,' said the man.

Hasan had been taking notes on the stories – he called them 'scientific notes' – though really he was doing little more than writing the titles of the stories down. It made him feel he was doing something positive to help the Giant. Hasan desperately wanted to know more about stories. His interest in them had sharpened since arriving in the Castle. Still, when the Giant tried to explain to him that if stories were not shared they would be lost, Hasan couldn't quite grasp what the Giant meant.

'But how can they be lost when they are stored in libraries throughout the world?' he asked.

'Their meaning will be lost, Hasan, the pleasure taken in them will be lost. There are thousands and thousands of musty old books crammed with stories, but have you ever tried to read those books? If stories are left unshared for centuries then the way they are written remains unchanged and they fall out of use through neglect. Stories must be shared if they are to stay alive.'

Hasan thought about this. 'I've one to share,' he said. 'It's about a scientist and an owl.'

THE HUMAN TONGUE

A SCIENTIST WHO WAS STUDYING NATURAL HISTORY WANTED TO know if owls were as wise as people made them out to be, and so he caught one in a trap. 'If you can tell me what is the best thing about human beings and what is the worse thing about them, I'll let you go,' he told it.

'The best thing about them is their tongues,' said the owl without a moment's hesitation.

This surprised the scientist. 'Why's that?' he asked.

'With the tongue human beings discuss all manner of things,' said the owl. 'With it they sing, and tell stories. They warn their fellows of danger, they comfort one another, they cheer up the sad, and share all kinds of fascinating knowledge.'

'And what is the worst thing about human beings?' asked the scientist.

'Their tongues,' said the owl, again without a moment's hesitation.

'How can the tongue be both the best and the worst part of a human being?' asked the scientist.

'Because they also use it to spread gossip, and to cheat,' said the owl. 'With it they plot murder and spread confusion.'

The scientist decided that the owl's reputation for wisdom was justified.

R ani had been busy rooting through all the shelves she could reach to see if she could find a copy of her favourite book. And there it was, lying flat on a bottom shelf with other illustrated books that were too large to stand upright – a child's version of the *Panchatantra*. Could the Giant possibly know all the stories it contained? she wondered. He was bound to know the grown-up versions of the stories, but maybe the writers of this particular version had secretly included some new stories. She flicked through the book, sighing with every familiar story she came to. *My Giant is too wise not to know them all*, she thought. But still, she had to tell them.

Once again she gathered the others together, and again they humoured her, allowing her to arrange them in the grouping she thought most suitable for story-telling.

THE BAND OF GOLD

Two magpies lived in the branches of an old tree, and in a hollow beneath the tree lived a cobra. This wasn't the best of arrangements as far as the magpies were concerned. Whenever they laid eggs the snake would slither up the tree and eat them. It was impossible for the magpies to start a family, and they couldn't move to another tree because the rest were occupied.

They decided to seek advice from a jackal who had a reputation for cunning. The jackal was no friend of the snake and was glad to help.

'A princess who swims in a lake at the edge of the wood each afternoon leaves her jewels on the river bank,' it said, 'and among the jewels is a band of gold. Simply steal it and drop it outside the snake's hole.'

'But we can't bribe him with a gold band,' said the magpies.

'I know that,' said the jackal. 'Just do as I say.'

The magpies flew off, and following the jackal's instructions snatched the gold band from where the princess had put it down on the river bank.

The theft caused such a great commotion that people from all over the area came rushing to the princess's aid. A search-party was quickly formed to hunt down the magpies, who in the meantime had dropped the gold band outside the snake's hollow. As fate would have it, the search-party discovered the gold band just as the cobra came out to investigate all the noise and kerfuffle. They killed the snake, skinned it, and left the remains at the bottom of the tree. The delighted magpies ate up the remains before flying off to thank the jackal for its advice.

'How on earth did you know the gold band was the thing to steal?' they asked.

'Any object can be used as a weapon if cunning is applied,' said the jackal.

Betts looked up from the little circle Rani had arranged. The Giant was shifting about uneasily. Every now and again he cocked an ear, listening to a noise only he could hear. With each passing moment his face looked more shrunken and care-worn.

'We're not helping him any, are we?' Betts whispered to Liam.

They moved across the room, whispering, while Rani, who was still engrossed in her book, began to tell other stories. They were surprised to see that Hasan had carried on sitting there, listening politely.

'Hasan's a bit weird, isn't he?' said Betts. 'On one hand he's questioning the Giant about the value of the stories, and at the same time he seems to love hearing them.'

'Maybe he's trying to work something out?'

'Like what?' asked Betts.

Liam looked back at Hasan and shrugged. He didn't have an answer.

WORRY

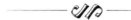

ONE DAY A CAT WHO HAD VERY CUNNINGLY DISGUISED
herself as a squirrel found two mice in a field. They both
looked worried. One mouse was lying on his back with his
paws up in the air and the other was standing on a stone holding a small twig.

'What on earth are you two up to?' asked the cat.

The first mouse said he had been told that the sky was
going to fall and crush the earth.

'That's ridiculous,' said the cat. 'And anyway, how could
something as tiny as you hold up the sky?'

'Well, I can hold up a small bit of it,' said the mouse defiantly.

'And what about you? What are you up to?' the cat asked the second mouse.

'I've been told that a terrible monster is going to come along. So I'm standing guard.'

'And you think you can defeat it with a twig?' asked the amazed cat.

'We are both extremely worried,' said the mice. 'In fact we are sick with worry. We've done nothing but worry for days.'

'You are both foolish to worry about everything you're told,' said the cat. 'Especially about things you have no power over and that are unlikely to happen anyway. You'd do better to worry about the things you know for certain.'

'What kind of things?' asked the mice.

'Things like the fact that cats eat mice,' said the cat, stepping out of her disguise.

—ᴡᴠ—

THREE OF A KIND

THREE MEN DECIDED TO SEARCH THE FOREST NEAR WHICH they lived to see if they could find anything of value. The forest was clammy and dense, and after two days of stumbling through the tangled undergrowth and wading across half-buried streams they were exhausted. They were about to turn back when, in a clearing, they found three elephant tusks. Scratched by thorns, bitten by flies, and dehydrated by the heat, the men had no strength left to drag the tusks home.

They decided one of them must return to the village to bring back enough food and water to revive them. They picked straws, and the man who picked the shortest straw returned home while the other two stood guard over the tusks.

As soon as he was out of sight his two companions decided that they would kill him on his return and share whatever fortune they got from the tusks among themselves.

A similar thought had also occurred to the third man. He added poison to some of the food he brought back from the village but before he could offer it to his companions they clubbed him to death.

It should have occurred to the men that they were three of a kind, but it did not. The two surviving men drank the water, devoured the food, then gathered the tusks together and set off for home. They didn't get far. Within an hour the poison had begun to work and within another hour they too were dead.

And so three dead men lay in the steaming forest among the tangled vines, and three tusks lay waiting to be discovered all over again.

—⁓—

'And it serves them right!' said Rani, closing her book.

'Remember they were very poor people, Rani,' said the Story Giant. 'Don't you think it should have been the people who would have bought the tusks from them who should have ended up dead in the forest?'

'No one should take elephants' tusks,' she said. 'Elephants are gentle. They are wonderful. They are giants, like you.' She opened the book again, and lowered her head into the pictures.

'Why were there were only *three* tusks in the forest, anyway?' asked Hasan. 'Why not four? Surely if two elephants had died in the clearing there would have been four tusks?'

The entire moral argument about hunting and tusks had passed over his head.

The Story Giant smiled at Hasan. 'Perhaps it had always been the fate of the three men to die that way,' he suggested. 'Perhaps Fate had seen no reason to provide a fourth tusk.'

'Fate should not have provided *any* tusks,' said Rani. She put aside the book from which she had been reading and opened another.

—◦◦◦—

DEATH AND THE
TRICKSTER'S NAME

DEATH ALWAYS WISHED TO KNOW THE NAMES OF THE PEOPLE and things that he took away.

One day he visited a trickster who was sitting at a gambling table playing cards in the back room of a club on the outskirts of London, and when Death asked him his name he refused to give it.

'I've hidden it away so well, you'll never find it,' the man boasted.

Death tried to coax the trickster into revealing his name, but the trickster was confident he had hidden it in a place where it would never be found. He turned his back on Death, and went on playing cards.

Death was furious. Off he went, looking for the trickster's name.

Death searched everywhere. He searched mountains and valleys. He looked under shiny stones in the beds of streams. He looked down rabbit-holes and examined the insides of beehives. He searched bank-vaults and attics, and went rooting in every cupboard and shoebox on the planet. The search took years, but still Death would not give up. What were years to Death?

Then one day Death finally got lucky.

On a very tiny island, one that hardly peeped above the waves, Death saw a great oak tree and began digging down into its roots. Among them Death found a box and in the box was a parcel and in the parcel was a swan's nest, and in the swan's nest sat a rabbit and inside the rabbit was an egg.

Death brought the egg out into the sunlight and warmed it, and soon enough it hatched. Out came a slimy little thing, something bald and blind, which Death nurtured, and fed seeds and water, and did all he could to keep alive. It grew into a beautiful green parrot.

Death sat patiently beneath the giant oak on the tiny island, and waited for the parrot to speak. When finally the parrot did speak, it knew only two words. Over and over again it repeated the trickster's name.

So Death returned to the place where the trickster lived, and knocked on his door.

—⁓—

'Do you have a name?' Rani asked the Story Giant.
'I've had many names down the centuries, Rani.' The Giant did not seem inclined to be any more forthcoming with his answer. Betts noticed this, and before Rani could pursue her line of questioning, she cut across her.

'That last story seems unfinished,' she said. 'I'm pretty sure what happened next: Death claimed the trickster. But something else might have happened. The trickster could have had another trick up his sleeve.'

'Yes, it could have been a double-bluff,' said Liam. 'The trickster could have left a false name inside the parrot.'

'Sometimes stories are meant to end with all their possibilities left floating in the air,' said the Giant. He had slumped down in his chair, but now he drew himself up again, trying to find a less painful position.

'Leaving stories floating in the air is a trick story-tellers have used for centuries. It makes listeners use their own imagination. I'll give you an example.'

THE UNFINISHED STORY

'There was an old canal up in the north of England that was deep and full of duckweed,' said the Story Giant. 'It had been out of use for many years. One day a child was walking along the tow-path that ran beside the canal when the skeleton of a tall woman in a raggy green dress rose from the water and beckoned the child.'

The image of a skeleton rising from the canal made the Giant's listeners uneasy. They waited for him to continue, but he remained silent.

'What happened next?' they asked eventually.

'Nothing happened,' said the Giant.

'Nothing?'

'Absolutely nothing.'

'That's unfair!' Betts cried. 'Something must have happened.'

'I told you, nothing happened. Not everything in life has a neat ending, and sometimes stories are the same.'

Hasan peered up from the depths of a gigantic leather sofa in which he was sitting scribbling notes and rubbed the end of his nose. ' Fine, but that particular story is simply unfinished, isn't it? Surely for stories to work they must have a proper ending?'

'I'm with Hasan, there,' said Betts. 'If people knew they were never going to know the end of a story, they wouldn't begin reading it.'

'Ah, my visitors are becoming authorities on stories at last,' smiled the Giant. 'Very good. Still, there are some stories you must make up for yourselves. Tell me, how would you have had it end?'

'I believe she was a very wise girl and ran home and was very safe,' said Rani. 'And the horrible skeleton stayed on the bottom of the canal.'

'I reckon she was dragged into the canal by the skeleton,' said Liam.

'Or maybe it had a very different ending,' said Betts. 'Maybe she heard a sigh rise from the canal and a voice whisper, "The hour has come, but not the child." How would that be for an ending?'

They were quiet after that. They found the odd little story even more disturbing because nothing much had happened in it. The story was still out there, still on the tow-path, waiting to complete itself.

'The meaning behind the story of the trickster and Death is clear, though,' said Hasan. 'All is as Allah wishes. None can escape their fate.'

The others turned and looked at Hasan. The glow from the Giant's fire lit his tubby little face as he peered over the edge of the sofa.

The Giant thought of what Hasan would one day become. He imagined all the boy's little traits knitting together and forming the stony-faced diplomat he would surely end up being. And he thought of his own imminent fate, and of the years that had piled up on him like flakes of snow.

DAME GOODY'S EYE

THERE WAS AN OLD ENGLISH WOMAN CALLED DAME GOODY
who spent her days bringing children into the world and
nursing them when they were sick. Late one snowy winter's
evening she was visited by a stranger, a horseman dressed
from head to toe in black. He begged her to come and look
after his child, as its mother was sick.

Emergencies don't only happen in the daylight hours and at
convenient times, and Dame Goody was used to such requests.
She packed a few belongings, clambered up behind the rider
and was soon racing through the night. Dame Goody knew
the countryside well, but the night was so dark and the horse
so fast she had no idea in which direction they were heading.

In time they came to the stranger's home, a remote cottage far out on moorland she did not recognize. The cottage was cosy enough. It was simply furnished and resembled many other cottages she had been called to. A peat fire smouldered in the grate, an oil-lamp hung from a beam, and the stranger's wife sat in bed nursing her baby as best she could. Her other children, all of whom seemed neat and well-scrubbed, sat in various parts of the room reading or quietly playing games.

The sick woman handed the baby over to Dame Goody, along with a tiny silver jar that contained an ointment smelling of almonds. 'If the child wakes, smooth both of its eyelids with this,' she instructed.

Dame Goody settled herself into the cottage, nursing the child, and helping the mother with any odd job that was needed.

Whenever the baby woke from sleep she dutifully followed the mother's instructions and smeared a little ointment on both its eyelids.

Dame Goody had never come across this practice in all her years of looking after children. The baby's eyes were healthy enough, and she had no idea why the mother insisted on its eyelids being anointed.

Her curiosity soon won out. On the last day of her visit, when no one was watching, she dipped her finger into the jar and smeared a little ointment on her right eyelid.

The moment she did this the cottage and its inhabitants seemed transformed. All the furniture in the room appeared to be made of gold and the little fire in the grate now hissed and burned with blue flames. The baby she held in her arms was no longer a red-faced cherub. Instead, its ears were pointed, its eyes were green, and its little rose-bud mouth curled open to reveal a set of sharp, pointed teeth. Instead of fine downy hair, centipedes scurried about on its bald skull. The stranger who had brought her to the house had shrunk to half his original size, and what had been his hands now resembled paws. The mother, too, was transformed. The bed she lay in was made of grass and the children gathered around her had hooves, not feet.

If Dame Goody closed the eye onto which she had smeared the ointment, all seemed normal, but the moment she opened it again the strange and appalling apparitions returned. The terrified woman knew her sanity and perhaps even her very survival depended on leaving the house immediately. She put down the child – or whatever it was she was holding – and hurried out into the night.

Dame Goody never opened her right eye again. She sealed it with candle-wax and kept it shut tight as the lid of a tomb.

—ᴍ—

W ould you call that a fairy-story or ghost story?' asked Rani.
'I wouldn't call it either. I'd call it a folk-tale,' yawned Liam, who suddenly felt unaccountably tired.

Betts felt the same. She stretched, twisting her neck from side to side, then flopped down into a chair.

Rani picked up her book and marched over to the library table. 'Animal fables are much better than ghosts,' she said, burying her nose in another of her stories. A moment later she was asleep, her head resting on an illustration of a fox.

Had she been able to turn and look behind her, she would have seen that all her companions had now fallen asleep too.

The Giant remembered old Goody. She was neither from a fairy-tale nor a ghost story, and the incident with the ointment had been true. He'd seen her out on the moor regularly a few centuries ago. The bit about her pouring wax into her right eye was false – she'd actually sewn the lids together.

He grinned when he thought of her. The foibles of the long-gone mellow with time.

He slid open the drawer of his desk and took from it a tiny silver jar. It was the one Dame Goody had dropped all those years ago as she fled the weird cottage. She had become the moor itself now, and he was still there, still caught up in the ebb and flow of stories and dreams.

Idly, he opened the lid of the little jar and wondered what he would see if he smeared some onto his eyelids, but the ointment had long mouldered away.

He tapped the jar gently on his desk and a few specks of luminous green dust spilled from it. He brushed them away with the palm of his hand. Soon he too would be brushed away ...

He cocked an ear and listened. Far off, he heard granite blocks tumble from the Castle's walls as the wind tore down the remaining ivy in the now-derelict courtyard. And then yet another stone crashed down, but from somewhere much closer at hand. The library vibrated with the force of it and in the corner of the ceiling a spider's-web of hairline cracks appeared. A mirror-image of them spread across the Giant's face.

The last great sleep had begun to settle upon him in earnest. Again he thought of the stories, and his efforts to keep them alive and vibrant. His mind swept the world for evidence of another custodian, but there were none. He alone knew all the stories, bar one. He alone listened to the night, filtering and siphoning its tales, casting the great net of his imagination over the skin of a sleeping world. And if there was no one like himself, what then? Could mankind exist without stories – without those little tadpoles that lay at the root of all imagination?

He wondered if he had been foolish to believe that the arrival of the children on this night of all nights was anything other than mere coincidence. What place could they possibly have in his own story? He knew it was something they also wondered, disappointed as they were that so far none of their own tales seemed to have been the one he was searching for.

And now keeping them woven into a single dream was sapping his strength. He found himself having to loosen the threads that bound them all together.

The children had not been aware of him taking Dame Goody's little ointment jar from his desk. They were there with him in the library still, yet at the same time their dreaming selves had briefly slipped into the dreams they might have dreamt without his influence.

Betts, in her dream within a dream, had left the Castle and was back in Los Angeles showing a boy who looked suspiciously like Liam around a film set.

Liam himself was out hunting on the moor.

Hasan was busy fighting off a group of terrorists who were attacking his father's embassy.

Rani, in her dream within a dream was back in her own country, in the hotel laundry where she worked, only now she was the supervisor and had a room with an electric fan all to herself.

Part Two

Hasan tossed and turned in his bed. For a moment his dreams were fragmented and confused, then they settled again as the Story Giant began to weave the children back into the one dream.

One moment he had been fending off terrorists who had smashed into his father's embassy, the next moment – with the skewed logic of dreams – he was walking up the vast stone staircase back towards the Giant's library. But now there was a chill in the air that had not been there before, as if all the doors and windows of the Castle had been thrown open to the night. There was also the odd feeling that the Castle was somehow not as solid as it had been.

It was something all the children felt as they re-entered the Giant's orbit, an awareness that settled on the edge of consciousness and that they could not pin down.

At the top of the staircase on a landing to the right of the Giant's library door Hasan saw Rani standing alone admiring a painting.

'It is beautiful,' she said.

Hasan didn't think so. The painting was of a woman sitting in front of a mirror at a table littered with powder-puffs and scent bottles. She was smiling, and reflected in a corner of the mirror was a bed on which a cat was curled up asleep.

'I think it's awful,' he said.

'It is not,' said Rani.

'Father has stuffed our home with endless expensive paintings, and they are all dull,' insisted Hasan.

'Perhaps his paintings are dull, Hasan. But this is a beautiful picture.'

'I've been surrounded by expensive paintings all my life, Rani,' he sighed, 'and that's probably the first you've seen. How can you judge it?'

'Do you know the story about the poor girl and the perfume?' Rani asked.

'No.'

'I thought not,' she said.

THE SCENT OF KNOWLEDGE

A YOUNG GIRL WAS IN THE HABIT OF COMPLIMENTING people whenever they wore a perfume she liked the smell of. She always seemed to know the name of each scent, however rare or expensive.

She was not born with this sense of smell, but as the years passed it became more and more acute, and in time she grew from being poor and obscure to being a world-renowned authority on scents. Her opinion was sought constantly. Fashion-houses invited her to create special perfumes for them. Famous film stars and models sought her advice.

In old age she was asked how, in her youth, she had been able to recognize and name even the rarest kinds of perfumes, especially when she had been so poor that she had never been able to afford any for herself.

'Did you read endless books on the history of perfume?' she was asked.

'No,' she would reply.

'Did you have a great teacher – a famous scent-maker perhaps?'

'No,' she would reply.

'Then was it a gift inherited from your parents?'

Again she would shake her head.

'Then how on earth did you learn so much more about perfume than all the people who wore it?'

'I collected the bottles they discarded,' she said. 'It was the scent from the empty bottles that taught me.'

Rani left Hasan to make what he would of the story and moved off in search of other paintings. Soon she found herself in the longest and most extraordinary corridor she had ever seen. It was the main artery of the Castle and was as wide as a street. The floor was laid with slabs of pink and blue marble and on the walls were countless oil paintings, all hanging askew and in varying states of decay. Massive piles of furniture and statues were scattered at random down a central aisle, and moonlight poured through row upon row of tall windows, the light so intense that every minute detail in the paintings was enhanced. In the spaces between the windows stood gigantic potted ferns, their yellowing fronds curling in the dusty air.

One painting in particular caught Rani's attention. It was of a wolf peering out from the edge of a wood, and beside it, wearing an expression of great calmness, stood a child. The painting was so lifelike that she imagined if she were to put out her hand and touch the canvas she would feel the rough bristles on the wolf's back.

'What's a child doing with a wolf of all things?'

Rani turned to find Betts sitting on the back of an old sofa.

'I ought to be scared of this place. You ever seen such a corridor?'

Rani shook her head.

'You think the Giant gathered all this stuff for real – or did he just dream it up? It's spooky.' Betts slid from the sofa and joined Rani in front of the canvas.

'What do you think of all this?' she asked. 'I mean all the stuff that's happening here in the Castle?'

'I am sad that we cannot find his story,' said Rani quietly. 'I am sad that he is dying.'

The simplicity of Rani's reply made Betts uncomfortable. She nodded towards the picture. 'That's like an illustration from a fairy-tale, isn't it?' she said.

'It should be a fox in the painting, not a wolf.'

It was Liam speaking. Hauled back from his own separate dream of hunting out on the moor he stood behind them, also looking at the painting.

'My dad's an artist,' he went on. 'When we first came over here from Australia we stopped off in Japan, and dad bought me a book of woodcuts. Actually the wood-cuts were really for himself. One of the pictures was very similar to that painting.' He walked closer to the canvas. ' I think it's a copy. The only difference is that the artist has swapped the fox for a wolf. It makes the picture more dramatic.'

'I bet there's a weird story behind it,' said Betts.

'Yes, there is,' said Liam.

GRATITUDE

A WOMAN RESCUED A BABY FOX FROM TWO BOYS WHO WERE tormenting it, and discovered a piece of broken glass in its paw.

She took out the glass, bandaged the creature's paw with a strip torn from her dress and let it go.

The cub's mother, who was hiding in the distance with her other three cubs, had seen what had happened and took note of the woman's kindness.

Summer and autumn passed, and that winter, when the snow lay frozen over the countryside, the woman's only child became terribly ill. A doctor who examined the child said he could make a potion to cure it, but that he was missing one essential ingredient – the heart from a fox.

This horrified the woman and her husband. The last thing they wanted was to harm another creature. However, their love for their child overcame all other considerations, and they decided to ask a local farmer for help. They thought he, if anyone, would know how to find a fox's heart. The farmer agreed to do his best but warned them he might not succeed.

The next day while the child's mother was baking bread in the kitchen and staring out at the moonlit snow, a peculiar stranger appeared at the back door. It was a woman. She hovered in the shadow cast by the trunk of a great sycamore tree and the child's mother could not see her face.

'I've come from the farmer,' said the stranger. 'And I'm meant to give you this.'

She left a parcel made of leaves and tied with grass in the snow beside the door, then she hurried away. Inside the parcel was a fox's heart.

The doctor was called back, and mixing the heart with other ingredients, he fed it to the sick child who improved immediately.

While they were celebrating their good fortune there was another knock, this time at the front door. It was the farmer, looking downcast. He said because of the cold and the snow no foxes were to be found and, try as he might, he had been unable to obtain the heart they needed.

'But you've already sent a messenger with the heart,' they said in surprise.

The farmer swore he had done no such thing. Together, they went to the back of the house and opened the door at which the peculiar-looking stranger had called.

There were no footprints in the crisp snow that covered the garden. But there were fox-prints. Two sets, one leading up to the door and another leading away again.

—w—

L iam wished he'd found Betts alone in the corridor. It would have been like meeting her in the courtyard all over again. He wondered how much older she was than him. It was probably only a few months – but it was hard to tell and he didn't dare ask. He remembered the smell of her in the courtyard. It was a warm and sleepy smell, and thinking of it made him feel awkward and reinforced his shyness of her.

'It's an amazing story,' she said. 'Don't you think so, Rani?'

But Rani was not paying attention. She was looking out of one of the windows, nose pressed to the glass. 'Are there any wolves out there?' she asked.

'On the moor? There were centuries ago, but not now. There are ghosts though,' said Liam.

JAN COO

THERE ARE FEW PLACES IN ENGLAND AS COLD AND BLEAK IN winter as Dartmoor. The valleys and tors are shrouded in mists, and the wind is bleak, whispering between ancient rocks and the burial mounds of forgotten tribes.

Trudging home one evening to the farm on which he lived, a young man heard a voice calling to him.

'Jan Coo, Jan Coo,' it whispered.

Jan stopped and shouted out into the darkness, 'Who's calling me?'

There was no reply. He heard only the sound of the trickling streams. But later, just as he was entering the farmhouse, the voice whispered his name again.

Thinking it must be his imagination, or a trick of the wind, he asked his two brothers to come out into the night to listen with him. Before long the voice called again. There was no doubting it was real.

And so it went on night after night. The voice would call out Jan Coo's name, and when Jan Coo shouted out in answer, it would stop, and silence would fill the bleak moorland night.

His parents and his brothers begged him not to respond to the call.

'If you ignore it then maybe whatever's calling will go away,' they said.

Jan tried, but the voice persisted and grew more and more urgent the longer he remained silent. The family soon changed their minds. They decided that perhaps after all it was best for him to answer, for whenever he called out to it, the voice stopped, giving them all a rest from the terror it inspired.

All through the winter, night after night, the voice called. And night after night Jan Coo answered. Not even the snow that fell and muffled all other noises could change the sound of the voice that called out to him.

Then one misty evening when the moorland rivers roared with melting snow, and Jan Coo and his brothers were returning from securing their flock of sheep, the tone of the voice changed. It became a rustling in the frozen grass, a rumbling among the granite slabs.

'Jan Coo,' it called. 'Jan Coo.'

This time, when Jan called out in response the voice did not stop. On and on it went, until Jan could bear it no longer, and before his brothers could stop him, Jan had followed the voice into the darkness.

His brothers searched for him in vain. They returned home to the farm, hoping that he might have made his way back before them, and as they walked the voice that had called out Jan's name so insistently faded, and sank back into the body of the moor.

In all their years living on the moor they never heard it again.

Nor did Jan Coo ever return.

—⁓—

'Is that a true story?' whispered Rani.

'No, it's not,' said Betts. 'Stop trying to spook us, Liam.'

But Liam couldn't resist it, even at the expense of seeming uncool.

'See over there, where the moor dips down to a small group of trees?' He pointed into the darkness. 'That place is a bit like Wistman's Wood.'

WISTMAN'S WOOD

A FARMER WHO HAD LEFT HIS WIFE AND BABY AT HOME while he went off to a fair near Wistman's Wood on Dartmoor was returning home one evening when his pony and cart were overtaken by four huge black hounds. These were followed by a rider, also dressed in black.

'What are you hunting so late?' the farmer called out after the rider.

'We've finished hunting for the night,' the hooded figure shouted back, and he tossed a parcel of rags to the farmer.

The farmer took the parcel home and unwrapped it by candlelight. Inside the parcel was his child.

'That's one sick story,' said Betts. She looked horrified and flounced off, leaving Liam and Rani alone at the window.

'It was not a nice story. You frightened us.'

'I'm sorry,' said Liam, and he meant it. 'You're the last person I'd want to frighten, Rani.'

'Because I am small? In my country, Liam, I see far more horror than you or Betts can imagine – remind me one day to tell you some of –' She stopped and looked down the corridor towards Betts, who had turned back on her heels, trying to say something to them. But a whistling noise, the sound of wind hissing through ruins, had scooped up her voice and it was lost in a babble of other sounds.

A fox barked, a lion roared, the sound of a drum rattled in the wind; an owl hooted, monkeys chattered, a skull spoke to itself. Then there was a great sigh of pain that sounded like the disembodied voice of the Story Giant, and all the noises ceased as suddenly as they'd arisen. A calmness, silent as snow, descended over the Castle and filtered into them.

They stood close together listening, Rani snuggled between Betts and Liam. A narrow door on the far wall sagged on its hinges and swung open, its bolt clattering down from the rotting wood that was no longer able to hold it in place.

They were looking into the little theatre Betts had seen when she first dreamt her way into the Castle, and it was from here the noises had emerged.

The roof-beams had collapsed, smashing the seats and leaving a gaping hole in a wall through which the moorland was clearly visible. The sight of the moor beyond the theatre and the babble of voices convinced them that they were witnessing the Castle's death-throes.

Betts turned to Liam. 'Remember what he told us when he first drew us together in the library?' she asked.

'That if he died the Castle would die with him?'

'Yes. And that's what's happening now.'

'I don't want it to happen!' cried Rani.

Betts hushed her and hugged Rani close as yet another stone tumbled down.

They retreated back the way they had come. There was a muskiness in the air, and a hundred varieties of decay they could almost taste on their tongues. Draughts blew brittle leaves across the marble floor and heaped dust into corners. Though the moon still shone on the windows, a century of grime had settled on the glass within moments, and the corridor was far gloomier than it had been. The painting of the wolf and child was hardly visible. The sofa on which Betts had sat now sagged wearily, its fabric frayed, its springs spilling out like entrails.

When they reached the landing where Rani had been talking to Hasan, Rani gave a gasp of disappointment. The picture Hasan had so disliked and over which they had argued was worm-eaten and blotched now, and in places the paint had flaked away. Mildew covered the beautiful face she had admired, as if inflicting it with leprosy.

Sitting below the painting on the landing was the Giant. He was hunched forward, shaking his head back and forth, his body rocking in distress as he looked down the grand staircase to the hall below. It was vanishing along with the rest of the Castle. The great oak door had collapsed outwards onto the moor, and crystal chandeliers had come crashing down from the ceiling, the broken glass spilling across the floor and glittering like ice in the moonlight.

As they watched, the Giant rose uneasily from the stairs, unaware that they were behind him. He swayed a little, drunk on pain, then steadying himself against one of the few remaining banisters, he moved back towards the library. He walked bent over, as if burdened by his great height, his arms held out at an angle like broken wings.

The children gave him a little time, then followed quietly after him.

The library appeared to be the least altered part of the Castle, kept intact by the Giant's will alone. The Giant seemed to have recovered some of his posture, though the children were shocked to see quite how suddenly he had aged. His face was gaunt, his cheekbones protruded from wafer-thin skin, and the irises of his eyes had opened wide seeking more light.

Hasan was standing beside him, agitated and confused.

The children fidgeted, looking at each other uneasily. Seeing their discomfort the Giant turned his back on them and stared into the fire, which was now no more than a few blackened cinders.

'Keep faith with me,' he said. 'The story might still be found.'

The wind hissed through cracks that had appeared in the library door, and it sounded to the Giant to be the voice of Dame Goody saying good-bye. Then, as a yet deeper pain spread through his body, the door itself began to warp and vanish, and there was nothing beyond it but a white, swirling mist.

As the mist began drifting into the room a sense of inevitability enveloped them all. Nothing was unusual in dreams, they felt, not even this.

Slowly, the Giant moved across the library to a moth-eaten tapestry which he pulled back to reveal a stone archway that led out on to the Castle's highest balcony. Instinctively the children began to gather up some of the books they had pulled down from the shelves during the long night.

Dawn was less than an hour away when they joined the Giant outside. At either end of the balcony broken-nosed gargoyles watched out over the moor, and in the centre was a long table and a scattering of chairs. Screwed into the walls above them were cast-iron oil-lamps that gave off only a little light.

The children dumped their books on the table and sat down, leaving a massive chair hewn from a single block of moorland granite for the Giant.

The sky was more full of stars that the world was of stories, and below them the moonlit moor rippled and whispered with nocturnal life.

The Giant rested back in his chair. 'You've some stories left,' he said. 'I can smell them on your skin.'

And so they each told what they feared would be the last stories of all, while hoping against hope that the one he did not know would be among them.

Rani opened a book at random and began to read.

THE MAN WHO LISTENED
TO THE LION

A TRAVELLER WENT INTO A CAFÉ TO ORDER FOOD ONLY TO discover that he had lost his wallet. A thief who was sitting at the next table offered to help him find it.

'I distinctly remember taking my wallet out and counting the coins as I walked along,' said the traveller, 'so no doubt it will simply be lying on the path a little way from here.'

As they set out to retrace the traveller's steps, they were warned that a lion was prowling the neighbourhood, but the need to find his money overcame the traveller's fear – just as the thought of stealing it from the traveller overcame the thief's fear.

'We'll just have to watch out for each other. Agreed?' said the thief.

'Of course,' said the traveller.

They were halfway between the two towns when, sure enough, the lion appeared. The thief saw it first. Without a word of warning to the traveller he scarpered to safety up the nearest tree, knowing full well its branches were strong enough to hold only one of them.

All the traveller could do was cover himself with earth, lie on the ground and pretend to be dead. The lion soon came sniffing around him. Either because it had already eaten its fill or actually did think the traveller dead, it did no more than nuzzle its snout into his ear before wandering away again.

As soon as the lion was gone the traveller brushed himself down and, ignoring the thief, set off alone.

'We must continue our search for the wallet!' called the thief, climbing back down the tree.

'Did you see the lion nuzzle my ear?' asked the traveller.

'Yes, and I was afraid for you,' lied the thief.

'Well, the lion whispered something to me,' said the traveller.

'It whispered to you? The lion?'

'Yes. It told me you saw it first and clambered up the tree without warning me. It also said that if I couldn't trust you with my life, how much less could I trust you with my money.'

FEAR

A SQUIRREL, A BADGER AND A CROW WERE BOASTING TO EACH other about how brave they were.

To decide who was really the bravest they agreed to visit a derelict house reputed to be haunted by a human ghost. The bravest would be the one who went furthest into the house.

The squirrel was the first to try. It scampered up the steps, nudged the door open, and peered into the living room. The room was musky and dim and smelt of humans. It was lit only by a narrow beam of sunlight entering through the broken shutters on the windows.

The squirrel was about to go inside when it saw a figure standing against the far wall. It rushed back down the steps, trembling. 'There really *is* a ghost there!' it exclaimed. 'I thought it was just an old story.'

Its friends asked the squirrel to describe the ghost.

'Well, it's not a human ghost,' said the squirrel. 'It was about my height, and had a bushy tail.'

The badger trundled up the steps next. Sure enough, it too saw something against the far wall of the room, and was back down even quicker than the squirrel. It said it too had seen the ghost. 'It was quite terrifying,' the badger said. 'But you were wrong about the bushy tail. It has white markings, and a snout like mine.'

'You're both cowards,' said the crow, but when it tried to hop into the house it got no further than the other two before fear overcame it.

The crow said the ghost had been black, and had a beak rather similar to its own.

The three friends hurried away from the old house, afraid and puzzled by how the ghost had managed to take on the shape of each of them in turn.

What they did not know was that against the far wall of the room there had been a large mirror. They had been looking at themselves, and the fear they had felt had been inside them, not inside the house.

—⟁—

THE CHICKEN THAT LAID A GOAT

A FARMER WHO HAD FALLEN ON HARD TIMES OWNED A VERY scrawny chicken.

A stranger who was passing the yard in which the man kept the chicken thought it would make a nice snack and offered to buy it.

'You'd never be able to afford this chicken,' said the farmer. 'It's worth a fortune.'

'Worth a fortune? That! Why, it's the scrawniest chicken that's ever lived. It must be at least ninety-nine per cent feathers! If I was *really* hungry it wouldn't even do for a snack.'

'It provides us with sheep and goats,' said the farmer, defensively.

'That's the most absurd thing I've ever heard,' said the stranger. 'It doesn't look as if it's got the energy to lay an egg, let alone provide you with sheep and goats.'

'Don't you be so sure,' said the farmer. 'The other week I invited some friends over for dinner and we were going to eat this very chicken. Fortunately it escaped. My wife and I had to chase it all over the village.'

'Why was its escaping fortunate?' asked the stranger, who was now more interested in hearing about the chicken than in eating it.

'Well, when the people who were coming to dinner saw us chasing after it, they realized they weren't going to get much of a meal, and so they sent over a goat. The same thing happened a few days later with a second lot of people we invited to eat with us, and when *they* saw how scrawny the chicken was they sent over a sheep. Tomorrow we are going to invite some new people to dinner and let the chicken escape again. Now, how on earth can you say it's of no value when it provides us so much food?'

R ani closed her book and pushed it away from her. She was on the verge of crying. The Story Giant had known all her stories.

'You've done your best, Rani,' said Betts, leaning across the table and taking her hand as Liam began telling the last of his own tales.

A GIRL IN THE RAIN

TWO BROTHERS WERE CAUGHT IN A STORM WHILE RIDING home through an area rumoured to be occupied by ghosts. The rain was torrential. Rivers had burst their banks, bridges had been swept away, waterlogged paths had vanished beneath mud-slides. The canopy of trees under which they rode offered little cover, and everything around them was misty and sodden.

Now, the ghosts in this land had a habit of sucking people dry in much the same manner that a spider sucks the innards from a fly, but in order to be able to do so, the ghosts had to hold their victims' attention by hypnotizing them. The brothers had heard these stories, and the thought filled them with horror as they trudged on through the falling rain.

Suddenly they saw a remarkable sight. Kneeling on a path ahead of them was the most beautiful girl either of them had ever seen. She was about sixteen and looked in such distress that the younger of the brothers dismounted and went to her aid. The girl explained she had been on her way home when the storm broke and in her hurry she had twisted her ankle. Now here she was, stranded and helpless in a land of demons. She gazed deep into his eyes, beseeching him for help. 'I've been here for two hours,' she said, 'and now –'

Before she could utter another word, the younger brother saw a flash of steel and, as if in slow motion, saw the girl's head fly from her neck. He watched it bounce down the sloping path, the ragged veins spurting a mist of blood. Horrified, he turned to his brother, who sat above him on his horse, sword in hand.

'She was a demon,' said the older brother.

'But how could you tell? How could you be so certain?'

He turned back to look at the head with a mixture of revulsion and longing. It had come to rest in a pool of rain-water. The eyes blinked uncomprehendingly in his direction, then clouded over.

'You saw only her beauty,' said the older brother.

'No, I saw much more. I saw her gentleness. I saw her face, kind and luminous. But most of all I saw how very sweetly she returned my gaze.'

'All in so brief a time?'

'Yes!'

'Then you must thank God she did not stare into your eyes any longer. If whatever was kneeling on the path had entranced you for another moment it would have hypnotized you and sucked you dry.'

Again the younger brother asked, 'But how can you be so certain that she was a demon?'

'How long did she say she had been stranded?'

'Hours.'

'You saw the torrential rain that fell about her?'

'Yes.'

'And the waterlogged path on which she knelt?'

'Yes.'

'And her beautiful silk dress?'

'Yes.'

'And her hair? Describe her hair to me.'

'It was long and black and –' The younger brother bit his lip, suddenly subdued. 'It was bone-dry,' he whispered, 'as was her dress. Everything about her was bone-dry, despite the falling rain.'

—ɯ—

THE TRICKSTER'S KNIFE

Two brothers who were professional thieves committed a murder that no one could prove. Their alibi was cast-iron, and when they came before a judge he had no option but to free them.

A friend of the man they had murdered, a trickster, immediately swore he would revenge his companion's death. But how? He himself was no murderer. He thought up one scheme after another, only to abandon them as flawed. It was only some months later that he hit upon what he thought might be the perfect plan.

He searched high and low for the most unusual-looking knife he could find. On one side of the blade he engraved the word 'Life' and on the other side, 'Death'. Then with the help of his murdered friend's wife he slaughtered a goat, and filling a bucket with its blood, they lay in wait on a country path the thieves were known to use.

Within hours the thieves came prowling down the path. The man drenched both his friend's wife and the knife with the goat's blood, and while she lay on the ground feigning death he stood over her, knife in hand.

Seeing him, the thieves immediately jumped to the conclusion that he had murdered the woman.

'Friends, don't judge me too hastily,' begged the trickster. 'I must have been out of my mind to kill her.'

'We won't tell on you,' said the first brother.

'Of course not,' laughted the second. 'Where's the profit in that? We'll blackmail you instead.'

'But I've no money,' said the trickster. 'Take the most precious thing I own instead.'

'Which is?'

'This very knife,' said the trickster. 'It has the power of life and well as of death. Surely you've heard of its legendary power? Look.'

He touched the woman's blood-soaked body gently with the knife, and she immediately sat up and yawned, as if waking from a deep sleep.

The thieves were astonished. Their eyes had already told them she was dead, and now here she was, very much alive.

'How does this magic work?' they asked.

'To kill a person with this knife you must use it with the word "Death" turned uppermost on the blade. If you regret what you have done you simply turn the knife over so that the word "Life" is on top, then you touch your victim with it again.'

The brothers took the unusual knife with its exquisitely engraved blade and studied it with admiration. Nothing, absolutely nothing, could have appealed to them more. They were so lost in admiration of the knife it did not occur to them that now the woman was alive again there was no way they could blackmail the trickster.

That evening curiosity got the better of one of the dim-witted thieves, and he decided to try out the fatal knife. Taking it out of the drawer in which they had left it, he crept up to his sleeping brother and, with the word 'Death' turned uppermost on the blade, thrust it deep into his heart. He then turned the knife over so that the word 'Life' was uppermost, and touched the corpse with it once again. Of course, nothing happened.

So it was that the trickster and his murdered friend's wife attended the funeral of one of the murderous brothers, and the execution of the other.

—⟍⟍—

SLAD, NOT VLAD

EARLY ONE EVENING A MAN WHO HAD BECOME DISORIENTATED
in a thunderstorm managed to seek shelter in the ruins of an
old farmhouse out on the moor. Unknown to him, the ruin
was occupied by a vampire. At midnight he was disturbed by
a noise in the cellar and on investigating was horrified to see a
stone slab rising effortlessly into the air and the vampire crawl
out of the coffin beneath it.

Not all vampires are intelligent, no matter what most people
think, and before the spectre could even speak, the quick-
witted man shouted, 'What is your name, puny demon?'

The vampire was thrown into confusion. He was not
accustomed to being shouted at by mortals.

'Vlad,' he stammered. 'My name is Vlad.'

'Then you are not the vampire I have been sent to destroy. Where is the vampire known as Slad?'

The frightened vampire said he knew of no other creature like himself – certainly not one called Slad.

'Vlad, Slad! Why do you all have such stupid names? You are all witless idiots!' shouted the man, getting into the swing of things. He huffed and puffed and fumed at the vampire for wasting his time. He was a wonderful actor. He berated the vampire for being so ugly and for smelling of bat-droppings and stale blood. Then he calmed down and said, 'Seeing as you are Vlad and not Slad, I will spare your life.'

The vampire was so stunned that he even thanked the man, who then turned and walked from the ruined farm as calmly as his trembling knees allowed.

Later that night a wolf came loping by and found the vampire cowering in a pig-sty.

'What the devil's the matter?' it asked.

'A great and fierce vampire-slayer found me and spared my life,' said Vlad.

'And what did this vampire-slayer look like?' asked the wolf, who was the more sensible of the two.

'Just like a mortal,' said the vampire.

'Then it *was* a mortal, you fool. You've been tricked.'

The vampire did not trust the wolf's opinion, but he hated the idea of being fooled. In order to save face, he set off with the wolf in search of the man.

They soon found him, but once again the man was quick-witted. Without so much as glancing at the vampire he rushed up to the wolf and shouted into its face, 'This is not the vampire I told you I would pay you to find me. I asked for Slad! Slad, not Vlad! This is Vlad!'

Before the wolf could react, the vampire – thinking the wolf had been about to betray him – tore out its throat. He dragged the carcase off into the darkness while the man, thanking Heaven for his quick tongue, hurried off in the opposite direction.

—ɯɯ—

Hasan was sitting a little apart from the others waiting his turn to speak. He had not been concentrating on Liam's stories and had lost the thread of the tales. For the briefest of moments his dreaming self had shifted focus and was now floating above the Castle's battlements, looking down on the balcony. There was the Story Giant, shrunken, old, nearing his end. There was Liam beside him, and Betts and Rani. And there he was himself, a closed book between his hands. *'Why am I dreaming of these people?'* he wondered.

'Why am I dreaming of a dying giant and a castle instead of the one person I ought to be dreaming of?'

'Hasan? Hasan!' Rani was calling him from across the table. 'Liam's finished,' she said. 'It's your turn.'

THE MAN WHO THREW AWAY
HIS CHILD

ONE DAY A WOMAN GAVE BIRTH TO A CHILD. IT SHOULD HAVE been a happy occasion but her young husband was furious. 'We're too poor to be keeping a child,' he said. 'We must get rid of it.'

His wife was horrified by the suggestion and begged him to change his mind. But the man was heartless. He thought the child would get in the way of his sole ambition, which was to be rich. One night while his wife slept, he took the baby from her arms and, walking to a beautiful but lonely place by the river, threw it in. Within days his wife had died of grief.

As the years passed, he wiped the memory of his young wife and the terrible thing he had done from his mind, and eventually, through lying and cheating, he accumulated vast wealth and so achieved his ambition. Because he had been cunning enough to keep all his evil doings secret, people even thought him a good man. He now felt the only thing he needed to make his life complete was a new wife and family. He met a woman remarkably like his first wife. He remarried, and in time she had a beautiful smiling baby.

The man was delighted. He carried the baby around town cradled in his arms, showing it off to his neighbours and boasting of how precious and beautiful it was.

One morning he decided to go for a walk along the riverbank and took the baby with him. By accident he found himself in the same lonely spot he had visited with such murderous intent in his youth, when suddenly the baby opened its mouth and said: 'This is where you threw me in the river all those years ago.'

Startled, the man lost hold of the baby and it fell into the river and was swept away.

Hasan looked around the table. The Giant sat motionless, with his eyes closed. He seemed not to be listening any more, but the others were staring at Hasan, horrified at the coldness and strangeness of his story. Before they could voice a reaction, he began another. It was one of two stories that he had overheard a servant telling her daughter in the garden of his father's house, in the days when he had been happy. He decided to tell both stories, as both contained meanings he had only begun to understand since being in the Giant's presence.

THE MAN WHO FOLLOWED
HIS DREAM

A MAN WAS SITTING IN THE GARDEN OF HIS SMALL HOUSE in Riyadh, wondering how on earth he was going to pay off his debts. He had no work, and he owed money to everyone. He was dozing fretfully in the shade of a date palm when suddenly he heard a voice say, 'If you wish to find your fortune you must go to Cairo.' Now Cairo was in Egypt, many miles away, but the voice was so compelling he decided to set off immediately.

By the time the man arrived in Cairo he had spent the little money he had and was reduced to begging in the streets. He was arrested and the next morning appeared before a magistrate.

Asked what he, a total stranger from another country, was doing begging and sleeping rough in Cairo, he told the magistrate about the voice he had heard, and about the advice it had given him.

'You are a very foolish man,' said the magistrate, but not unkindly. 'That dream's a common dream. It is the kind all men have. Why, even I, a sane and practical man, once had the same dream.'

The man was astounded. 'You mean a voice told you that you would find your fortune here in Cairo?' he asked.

'Certainly not,' laughed the magistrate. 'In my dream it was your home city of Riyadh that was mentioned. Why, my dream was even more vivid than your own. I distinctly remember how in the dream a voice told me to dig beneath a date palm that grew in the garden of a small pink house beside a drinking well. But I wasn't stupid enough to leave everything behind to do so.'

The man realized immediately that the house the magistrate had described was in fact his own little house, and when the magistrate freed him he returned home as fast as he could. He dug up his garden, and sure enough, beneath the date palm the magistrate had mentioned, he found a heap of gold.

From that moment on, whenever he was asked which he thought the most important, money or knowledge, without a moment's hesitation he would say knowledge. For he knew that without the knowledge he had received by following his dream, the gold would never have been found.

—⁓—

WEALTH

A POOR MAN ASKED HIS FRIEND THE MISER IF HE COULD TAKE
a peep at the fortune the miser had stored away.

'With the greatest pleasure,' said the miser, and took him
along to the bank-vault in which he hoarded his money.

They sat in front of the vault staring through the bars for
hours, both enjoying the sight.

After a while the poor man asked, 'How long have you
spent acquiring all this wealth?'

'All my life,' said the miser.

'And what do you intend to do with it?' asked his friend.

'Do with it? Why, nothing at all,' the miser replied.
'Having spent all my life accumulating it, why on earth

should I squander it now that I'm old?'

The men lapsed into silence again and continued to stare at the vault, lost in admiration.

'Tell me,' said the miser after another hour or so had passed, 'why do you think we have remained such good friends all these years?'

'Because we are both so incredibly poor,' his companion sighed.

'Poor! But I have all this wealth!' said the miser.

'Yes,' replied his friend, ' but you are no more able to spend it than I.'

As Hasan finished his story a solitary bird, one whose song he did not recognize, called hesitantly out on the moor. The children listened to it in silence, and all felt the same crushing sense of defeat. Surely it was too late to find the Giant's story now? Betts started on her stories regardless. And still the Story Giant sat motionless, his head sagging towards the table as if bowed in prayer.

MRS BEPPO'S MAGIC BAG

A WOMAN CALLED MRS BEPPO BOUGHT A BAG IN A FLEA-market. It was a large bag with a strong leather strap and she decided it would be perfect for her shoplifting expeditions.

Usually little old women are seen as sweet and helpless and while Mrs Beppo was little and old, she certainly wasn't sweet or helpless. She was vindictive, quarrelsome and a terror to everyone. Her children left home the moment they could and were as glad to see the back of her as she was of them.

After her first shoplifting expedition with the new bag, Mrs Beppo returned home quite satisfied with her day's work, but when she tipped up the bag she found it was empty. Everything she had put inside it had vanished. Mrs Beppo examined the bag and discovered a label inside it that read,

'All the things you wish in here
Will without fail disappear.'

'Well, I'll be,' she said. 'No wonder everything's vanished.'

The horrid little woman decided to test the bag out on her next-door neighbour's cat. Hurrying to the bottom of the garden where the cat was dozing on the wall, she opened the bag and called, 'Here pussy, pussy, in you get.'

Immediately the startled cat flew off the wall and into the bag and when Mrs Beppo peered into it, there was nothing to be seen.

'The bag's endless,' she thought. 'I can wish anything inside it.'

And she could. If anyone she owed money to called on her she would wish them inside the bag and they'd promptly vanish, along with her debt. If she got caught shoplifting, in would go the store-detective. Any major trouble and in would go policemen and judges and entire courtrooms.

If Mrs Beppo had stuck to figures of authority, against whom most people have one grudge or another, this mightn't have been so bad. But she even wished away tiny babies who annoyed her by crying, and quite a few of her elderly neighbours vanished mysteriously as well.

She soon discovered she could put absolutely *anything*

inside the bag, and things like illness, hunger and pain miraculously vanished from her life. But Mrs Beppo only put things in as they affected her. She could not be bothered with other people's unhappiness or pain. And the million-and-one things she might have done to make the world a better place remained undone.

Her most remarkable discovery, though, was that she could put Death inside the bag, as she found out when he came calling for her at four o'clock one winter's morning. He stood at the edge of her bed with his scythe and black hooded cloak, and she simply hooted with laughter, opened the bag, and shouted, 'Death, Death, in you get!'

Unfortunately for Mrs Beppo, she had been using the bag so much it had become a little worn in places and Death managed to slip out of a hole. When she realized this she quickly stitched it up again and checked it thoroughly for any more threadbare patches. Then she went looking for Death to put him back in.

But Death was no fool. He knew this would be the first thing she would do, so he lay in ambush for her one night and grabbed her while she was off-guard.

And so it was that Mrs Beppo died and found herself heading towards Hell, still clutching her remarkable bag. As she came near that hot place she decided it was not at all to her liking and so she opened the bag and called, 'Hell, Hell, in you get!' Immediately a great howling and stench of sulphur filled the atmosphere and Hell vanished into Mrs Beppo's bag.

Mrs Beppo turned round and in less than a blink found herself standing outside the Gates of Heaven. It seemed to take no time at all because, in terms of physical distance, the two places are not all that far apart.

There was an Angel standing outside the Gates but because she'd been such an awful person he refused to let her in.

'But there is nowhere else to go!' she complained. 'Hell's been swallowed by my bag. If you cause me any bother, I'll have it swallow up Heaven as well!'

'I doubt that,' said the Angel. 'Heaven and Hell are the two things the bag cannot swallow.'

'But it can! I saw it swallow up Hell with my own eyes!'

'That was everyone else's Hell,' said the Angel. ' Your bag cannot swallow Heaven or Hell for the simple reason that each person makes their own Heaven and their own Hell. For you, Hell is now being unable to get into either.'

Mrs Beppo dimly understood the logic of this. She knew there was only one place left to go. She opened the bag and cried, 'Mrs Beppo, Mrs Beppo, in you get!' and then she vanished.

—⟋⟍—

There were only two stories left for the Giant to hear, but he was hardly aware of the children now. His mind was drifting away, back to whatever his beginning might have been. He saw the cities of old Europe shake with the dull thud of bombs. He witnessed the looting of churches and the burning of monasteries. He saw hordes of barbarians sweeping down across the steppes. Back and back he drifted, his stories slipping away from him, lost in the currents and eddies of time. He saw wheatfields shiver in the heat of great famines and turn to dust. He watched the mysterious empire of the Aztecs vanish beneath a sea of sacrificial blood. He watched himself standing amongst the ruins of civilization after civilization. He was standing in a desert seeing the first pyramid rising from the sand.

Back and back his mind drifted. He saw the first story fall from the heavens like a shooting star ...

As Betts told the last stories the darkness began to melt away from the moor. Moss-covered boulders and an ocean of purple heather rose from the sameness of the night. Other birds were singing now, turning the moor into a vast auditorium, and above the battlements hovered a kestrel that only Liam noticed. He watched the bird, imagining it to be the Story Giant's soul taking leave of them.

DEATH AND THE POET

AN OLD POET WAS SITTING AT HER TABLE WRITING WHEN DEATH
slid in under her door and demanded her soul. The poet was not
ready to die and asked if she could have a few more years, as life was
quite pleasant for once. Death was in two minds, but the woman
knew he was a compulsive gambler who could not resist a bet.

Her house was on a cliff overlooking the Atlantic Ocean
and she could tell that a storm was imminent. 'Let's have a
wager on which is the stronger, a tree or grass,' she suggested.
'And if I win, give me the few years I crave.'

'Fine,' said Death, 'but as you've suggested the bet, it is
only right that I get first choice, and I choose the tree as being
the stronger.'

Death had hardly spoken when the storm the poet had seen gathering out on the ocean broke. They sat together in the kitchen and listened as torrential rain fell and the wind howled and rattled the little house. By dawn the storm had moved on, and once again the little house and the land around it was mouse-quiet.

Death opened the kitchen door and stepped out into the garden. On the lawn lay a giant tree, its branches snapped by the wind, but the grass glittered with rain-drops; washed clean and undamaged, it looked as fresh and green as ever.

So the poet was granted the extra years she wished.

When her time was up her visitor came again, and again sat with her in the kitchen, still unable to resist a bet.

It was a hot summer's day this time, and the fierce sun shone down on the garden with a merciless heat. When the poet asked the same question: 'Which is stronger, a tree or grass?' Death thought, 'I'll not be tricked a second time,' and chose grass.

But this time when Death opened the door and stepped outside into the garden he saw how the trees were crowded with blossom and alive with the hum of bees, but the grass had withered in the sun's heat.

And so yet again the old poet had won her bet, and once more was granted the years she craved.

When Death came a third time he found her in her tiny bedroom, books piled up neatly, letters addressed to friends waiting on the mantelpiece. Everything tidied away. This time she did not suggest a wager.

This time she said, 'I'm ready now. Welcome, Death.'

—◊—

THE OWLS THAT COULD NOT SEE
BEYOND THE RUINS

A KING WHO LOVED FALCONRY WENT OFF TO FIGHT A BATTLE in a distant land and left behind him his favourite hawk. The bird perched itself high up in the ruins of a castle the king had long abandoned in favour of a magnificent palace.

From the top of a tower glued together with ivy, the hawk could see the entire kingdom, and here it awaited its master's return, and each hour that passed was an hour of longing.

The shadowy ruins beneath it were now inhabited by owls. They nested in the crumbling eaves and swooped nightly through the dim light in search of moths and voles and scurrying mice. The hawk's arrival had thrown them into confusion.

They believed it had come to take over the ruins.

'I live in a palace and rest on the arm of a king,' said the hawk. 'Why would I swap such privileges to live in a ruin?'

The owls were not convinced. For them, the ruins were as near paradise as they could imagine. How could another bird not think the same? They called a Council of Owls to decide what to do about the hawk.

'Bribe him with a juicy, fat rat,' said one.

'Or a dozen young mice,' said another.

'Give him an abundance of voles,' said a third.

'Offer a retinue of moths,' said a fourth.

All in a panic, all forgetting a hawk could plunder a fat baby lamb at will!

The owls were divided on how best to deal with the hawk, and the longer it perched on the tower the more alarmed they became.

Some suggested attacking the owl all together, others suggested making it their lord. None could see the truth of the matter – that the ruins were inconsequential to the hawk.

It was not long before they broke into factions and began to argue among themselves, and sure enough their arguments turned into war. Each night there were skirmishes or full-blown battles, and each dawn the survivors retreated bleeding, blinded and broken-beaked back to their crumbling eaves.

The hawk was all but oblivious to this, and when the king returned triumphant from his wars, it rose from the tower, and with a flick of its wings was gone.

———〜〜———

Hasan had stopped listening to the stories. There had been too many about death. *What did they know of it?* he thought. He looked out across the moor, and as a thin line of light began to illuminate the horizon, he realized that dawn was only moments away. He felt as if he was floating away from the others, and soon their voices had become muffled and indistinct. After a while he found himself down below the Castle on the soft moorland grass talking to a woman he loved as he could love no one else. A woman who had tried so hard not to desert him by dying, but who had failed.

'Why aren't you coming home, mother?'

'I'm sitting here forever, Hasan.'

'But it is not your country.'

'No country is mine now, Hasan.'

'Father has a mistress now.'

'To which he is welcome, Hasan. Hasan, do you miss me?'

'Yes.'

'Kiss me, then.'

And he tried to kiss her, but she was gone. There was only the sound of the wind shaking the bracken and sobbing into the open mouths of the rabbit-warrens.

The Giant watched from the balcony, and as fatigue ate into his bones, he became aware of Hasan unravelling from the communal dream.

The stone archway leading from the library out onto the balcony began to corrode and give way. The Castle's trauma was nearly over, its disintegration almost complete.

Liam, Betts and Rani had stopped speaking and were watching the Giant intently.

He lolled back in his chair, paying them scant attention, his ashen face caving in upon itself, his great knotted hands fluttering with pain. Then, as dawn finally spilled over the horizon and flooded the balcony with light, he lost all hold over the children and they began to unravel from the dream of their own accord.

All longed for one more story to be told. But it was too late.

Liam heard the bark of squabbling fox-cubs and the gentle lapping of water. He faded. Rani heard the clamour of rickshaws; then she, too, was gone. Betts confused the rising sun with the red-and-blue glow of the neon lights she hated so much, then she vanished along with the others.

The Giant was alone on the balcony. He thought, *Soon everything will look the same: the moor, the Castle, myself. A valley here, a hill there, graduations of colour and texture, a few tell-tale signs, but overall it will be as if I had never existed.*

He knew then that there would always be a story unknown to him, one he was not meant to know. Four thousand years of stories and dreams weighed down on his eyelids. He exhaled, and a great sleep overcame him.

Dawn broke, and the rising sun made the dome of the mosque that dominated the view from Hasan's bedroom window appear to be decorated with an even deeper gold. As the first of the day's five daily prayers was intoned from the top of the minarets, down on the lawn between the tall cypress trees the house-servants unrolled their mats and knelt towards Mecca to join in the prayer.

Hasan sat on the edge of his bed and touched his cheek. It felt cool and wind-blown, as if he had actually been in the place about which he had dreamed. He had never experienced so realistic a dream. Parts of it had already faded, but he distinctly remembered a giant, and a landscape that had been totally alien to him in which had stood a remarkable castle.

He tried to recall other things. There had been stories, some of which he had related himself, and there had been other children. He had been aloof from them, protecting himself in a shell of stiff formality, but he had liked their company. Had they liked his company? He doubted it. Hasan was not good at making friends.

What he remembered vividly was that the strange giant had been sitting at a table out on a large stone balcony. And he remembered him dying. That was the horrible bit of the dream. He had muddled the Giant and his mother together. Also in the dream there had been something left unfinished. He hated things to be left unfinished, he hated loose threads. In real life he had lost his mother before they had had time to say a proper goodbye, and she would be a loose thread forever, someone eternally beyond his reach.

Hasan began to cry. For his mother, for the Giant, for his aloofness with the children who might have been his friends, for himself. He wished he could dream his dream all over again.

Waking, Betts had instantly forgotten the other children. She remembered an awful woman running around trying to catch Death inside a bag, and a talking skull and – yes! – somehow Brer Rabbit had been in the dream, but it was all fuzzy stuff. The only thing she remembered clearly was trying to find a story no one knew. Weird. She dressed and walked into the kitchen where her mother, still only half-dressed, was sitting at a table nursing a cup of strong coffee and smoking a cigarette.

By the time Betts had finished breakfast and was on the bus to school her entire dream was forgotten. But there came a moment when something jogged her memory. That afternoon on the wall of a classroom she'd been passing she'd seen the picture of a boat, and had suddenly formed an image of a boy she imagined she knew but couldn't place. Curly hair, sullen, huddled inside an oversized duffel coat.

Liam lay on his bunk and watched the light reflecting up from the river onto the cabin ceiling. There were a number of jobs he had to do that morning, and the first and foremost of these was to splice some rope that had become tangled in the boat's propeller and been chewed to bits.

Splicing was basically weaving together the threads of two separate ropes to make them into one. The job had been on his mind before he'd fallen asleep the previous evening, and he'd woken with the thought of weaving in his mind. Had he dreamed of weaving rope? Liam never remembered his dreams. They said that everyone dreamed, but he was sceptical about that. He'd only ever remembered two or three in his entire life.

Rani woke to the cawing of crows and the cloying scent of marigolds heaped up in a pile below the wrought-iron balcony on which she'd slept. The marigolds had been gathered by her uncle who was taking them down to the burning-ghats at the river's edge, where they would be used to decorate the funeral pyres. Death was not a hidden thing in the society in which Rani lived. She often saw families carrying the shroud-wrapped bodies of their loved ones to be consumed by flames, the stretchers bedecked by woven bouquets of marigolds.

Today was no different. She passed two funeral processions on her way to work at the hotel laundry, and returning home that evening along a cobbled lane beside the river had seen smoke rising from the burning-ghats. Usually these sights hardly impinged on her consciousness, so common were they, but today they were charged with extra significance. She felt the way she did because of her dream the previous evening. It had begun wonderfully with a fairy-tale castle and had ended sadly with an incident she could not recall. One thing that had stood out in her dream was a fat little boy who was always seeking attention. She had actually grown to like him.

Now it was night again, and again Hasan's father was absent, leaving him in the company of the house-staff. But tonight he did not beg to stay up. Tonight as soon as supper was over he went straight up to his room and climbed into bed. He lay in the darkness, lulled by the slow hum of the air-conditioning. He visualized everything he could about the previous evening – the Giant, the Castle, the moor – and he attempted to will himself back into the same dream.

But of course it was not quite the same dream. Nothing is ever repeated exactly as it happened. As he fell asleep Hasan remembered how his mother had vanished when he had attempted to kiss her cheek the night before ...

And now here she was again, in a different dress this time, walking across the soft moorland grass towards him.

'You're back, Hasan. How lovely. Come, sit beside me. Do you remember how you were at school in Switzerland when I suddenly took ill?'

How could he forget! He had not been beside her in her final moments. He had not been able to kiss her goodbye.

'Of course I do,' he whispered.

'And no doubt you blamed yourself when you were unable to come home in time. Tell me, Hasan, did you imagine I would be in pain – crying because I thought you had abandoned me?'

He nodded, 'Yes.'

'And you also thought that I had abandoned you?'

It was exactly what he had thought. And his grief had been so great that he had been unable to bear feeling it for long. He lacked a way of dealing with it, and so had closed his emotions down.

'Silly boy, how could I ever abandon you? You've always been with me, here –' she tapped her heart '– even since before you were born. Nothing can separate us from the love we share, Hasan, not even death. I knew I would see you again. It is part of our story, my love.'

'I wanted to kiss you goodbye.'

She smiled a radiant smile and patted her cheek with a finger. 'Then do so now, darling.'

Hasan hugged her and smelt the scent of peace he had always associated with her. Then he said the special goodbye he had needed to say for so long.

'And now, sweetheart, you must begin to live your life again,' she said.

His mother's ghost stroked his hair and then was gone. And with her vanished his immense confusion and the terrible feeling that they had betrayed one another. Hasan might have woken then, or drifted into a far simpler sleep, but he was back in the Story Giant's province, and part of his sleeping mind knew there was something else he might achieve.

His dreaming self stood among the ferns and gorse, calling out to the other children he knew had been here in this very place. He was elated now that he had made his peace with his mother. 'Liam,' he called. 'Rani! Betts!'

In dreams the laws of the physical world do not apply, and time and space can be manipulated according to the dreamer's will. Caught up in the ebb and flow of time, Hasan's voice drifted across the continents. Betts, Rani and Liam heard him calling. His voice entered their own slumbers, bright and clear, and they knew with the certainty of dreams what Hasan wanted. The children wove one another back into a single dream; and then they were together again on the moor.

Only there was neither Story Giant nor Castle now. There were a few broken walls and blocks of granite scattered about, and indentations in the earth that suggested where the Castle might have stood, but nothing else.

They were standing on a ridge above a gently sloping valley. Betts, Liam, Rani and Hasan. In a wood below them a screech-owl called its mate, and nearer at hand a couple of moorland ponies snuffled and stomped the earth in their sleep. The wide sky above them was cloudless and the full moon covered the entire moor in a bright silver light.

Betts looked from one horizon to the other. 'It's as if he never existed,' she sighed. She put her arm around Rani, who had come to stand beside her.

Rani also sighed, imitating the older girl. 'It's horrible that he never got to know his story,' she said. 'And all those wonderful things he told us. Will we remember any of them for long?'

Liam paced disconsolately about, prodding the earth and turning over stones with his foot while Hasan fiddled with the notebook he had carried about with him in the Castle. He held it at an angle, the better to read it by moonlight.

'I made some notes of the things he told us,' he said. 'One of the things was that stories must be shared if they are to stay alive. Then later –' he flicked through his notebook '– then later he said, "There are some stories you must make up for yourselves."'

'Then that is what we must do,' said Rani, solemnly. 'We must make up a story for him, in his honour.'

The moment Rani spoke, a shock of understanding passed through Hasan.

It was an electric charge, a truth as simple as it was profound.

'We are the story he does not know!' he shouted. 'It's the story of his death and of our returning here! He could never have known it because he had to die before it could be told!'

The children were stunned. It was so obvious.

'Then let us tell the story the best we can,' whispered Rani. 'Come, let us sit down in a circle, as it should be done.'

They sat on the mossy ground and they told their story.

Hasan began. 'Once upon a time,' he said, 'there was an overweight young boy.'

'And a street-wise girl,' said Betts.

'And a boy who loved rivers and foxes,' said Liam.

'And a young Indian girl for whom stories were an escape,' said Rani ...

THE STORY GIANT

… AND THEY ALL DREAMED OF A CASTLE FAR OUT ON AN ISOLATED MOOR. And in this castle lived a giant who was over four thousand years old and in his mind and all around him were stored the most wonderful stories in the world. But there was one story missing, and he did not realize that he was part of it. Then one day the Giant died and his castle fell apart, and all the stories he had gathered began to die with him. But the children realized that they had the power to bring the Giant back into existence.

Together they willed the ruins to re-form. Moss shrank away from the moor to reveal slabs of marble, and once again the Castle's entrance hall appeared before them. The stone arch Betts had noticed when she'd first entered the Giant's library appeared from under the grass, and for a second time she read the inscription carved into it: *The light of imagination transcends decay.* Doors, windows and chandeliers materialized out of thin air. Broken, time-pitted columns righted themselves. Walls and staircases pushed up out of the earth like livings things. Then there it was again, whole and as it had been before, the Story Giant's Castle.

And just as the dawn broke and wakefulness began to pull the children apart, to their delight they saw up on the balcony above them a tall figure, transparent at first, then growing more and more substantial, take shape before their eyes and...

The Story Giant woke and sniffed the air. Children had come again.

—ᨳ—

If it is of interest to anyone, although it is all but impossible to find under normal circumstances, the Story Giant's castle is situated on Dartmoor, in the vicinity of Widecombe-in-the-Moor. Though they have now left the area, the boat Liam and his father lived on was moored not too many miles away in Dittisham Mill Creek on the River Dart. Rani now works as an assistant librarian in Mysore, while Hasan had followed in his father's footsteps and is currently working in a foreign embassy somewhere in the Middle East. The whereabouts of Betts Bergman is not known.

—ᨳ—

SOURCE NOTES

Stories appear in different cultures dressed in different costumes, and travel without passport across borders and time. We can source the 'sources' back into antiquity and still not arrive at an 'original' source. For example, there are Irish folk-tales that have been traced back hundreds of years only for it to be discovered that they originated as Japanese folk-tales. The same with those gathered by the Grimm brothers. By the time of Wilhelm Grimm's death in 1859, stories he had fondly imagined to be of ancient Germanic origin were discovered in far older Sanskrit, Hebrew and Arabic texts. With such tales, some dating back thousands of years, there is an ongoing process of regeneration.

Some of the stories that appear in *The Story Giant* are straightforward retellings. With others I've taken the opening idea and expanded it into an entirely different version of the story. A couple are close adaptations and a few are more or less new stories, inspired by a few lines of poetry or by a single incident in a folk-tale. When stories are retold the emphasis often changes according to the times in which the story-teller lives. For example, in the source story from which 'When Immortality Was Lost' was adapted, the traveller is not an angel in disguise nor does he have a jar containing immortality – he is a traveller with a camel, and when the camel is stolen his hosts are ashamed and go in search of it. The emphasis is on their shame at not protecting their guest – 'immortality' does not enter into it. Below are some of the main sources used for my own retellings.

The Man Who Killed Two Thieves With a Chicken – adapted from a section extracted from 'Si' Djehas Miracles', *Arab Folktales*, Pantheon Books, New York

The Little Monster That Grew and Grew – after Æsop. Hercules and Pallas

How Wars Begin – after Jalaluddin Rumi, 16th century Sufi mystic

The Tramp and the Outcome of War – adapted from a fable in the *Panchatantra*

When Immortality Was Lost – adapted from a story from Morocco, source: *Arab Folktales*, Pantheon Books, New York

Supremacy – suggested by an Æsop fable

The Difference Between Heaven and Hell – adapted from a story in *Dragon's Tale, And Other Animal Fables of the Chinese Zodiac* by Demi, Harcourt Brace

John and Paul – old folk-tale current in many cultures

The Man who Bored People to Death – Joseph Jacobs, *Celtic Fairy Tales*, Senate

The Spirit Foxes – adapted from *Myths & Legends of Japan*

Hope – suggested by a fable from the *Panchatantra*

The Clothes That Were Invited to Dinner – there are many versions of this popular story in Arabic literature. Best known as a Djuha story, a version is also found in *Grimm's Fairy Tales*

A Simple Trick – traditional Djuha story

Degrees of Sorrow and Happiness – traditional Djuha story

The Shadow – adapted from Æsop

A Handful of Corn – adapted from *Arab Folktales*, Pantheon Books, New York

The Lamp – two Djuha stories combined

The Place Ahead – told to me by a friend

The Monster in the Desert – sources: Robert Creeley's *Presences*, Scribner's, New York, 1976. Also Eugene Watson Burlingame's *Buddhist Parables* (Yale University Press, 1922) as mentioned by Joseph Campbell in *The Hero With a Thousand Faces* (Fontana Press, 1993)

The Dragon-Slayer's Mum – suggested by a legend in *Albion, a Guide to Legendary Britain,* Paladin

Tiddalik the Frog – adapted from a story in *The Dreamtime: Australian Aboriginal Myths,* Rigby Limited, Adelaide, 1965

The Owl's Trick – adapted from Æsop

Brer Rabbit and the Alligator – *Nights With Uncle Remus, Myths and Legends of the Old Plantation*, 1883; also *The People Could Fly, American Black Folktales*, Alfred A. Knopf, New York

The Talking Skull – *There was a Certain Man (Spoken Art of the Fipa)*, Clarendon Press, Oxford

Man is Cunning, Cunning is Man – traditional Arab folk-tale, but widespread, with Indian and African versions

The Tongue – Æsop's master Xanthus asked him to prepare his dinner-guests good meat one day and inferior meat the next. On both days Æsop provides tongues.

A Band of Gold – the *Panchatantra*

Worry – from memory, source unknown

Three of a Kind – *Congo Stories for Young Children*, Stirling Tract Enterprise, 1950s. Also echoed in Chaucer's 'The Pardoner's Tale'

Death and the Trickster's Name – suggested by a paragraph in Robert Creeley's *Presences*, Scribners, 1976

Dame Goody's Eye – Joseph Jacobs, *English Fairy Tales*, Penguin Classics; first published in *English Fairy Tales* and *More English Fairy Tales*, 1890, 1894

The Scent of Knowledge – suggested by Æsop

Gratitude – *Tales of Old Japan* by Freeman-Mitford, 1871; also found in *Myths & Legends of Japan,* Harrap & Co, 1913

Jan Coo – Legend found in *Albion, a Guide to Legendary Britain*, Paladin; first told by William Crossing in *Tales of the Dartmoor Pixies* (1890)

Wistman's Wood – Devonshire legend, as above

The Man Who Listened to the Lion – versions in both Æsop and the *Panchatantra*

Fear – Indian, but widespread

The Chicken That Laid a Goat – *Stories From the Arab Past*, Hoopoe Books, Cairo; versions also found in Djuha stories and others

A Girl in the Rain – adapted from *The Prince and the Badger, Tales of Old Japan*, by Freeman-Mitford, 1871

The Trickster's Knife – adapted from a section extracted from 'Si' Djehas Miracles', *Arab Folktales*, Pantheon Books, New York

Slad, Not Vlad – suggested by Æsop and others

The Man Who Threw Away His Child – suggested by a Chinese tale

The Man Who Followed his Dream – *One Thousand and One Arabian Nights*

Wealth – suggested by Æsop

Mrs Beppo's Magic Bag – suggested by stories of someone trapping the Devil or Death in a box or bag, or getting into Heaven, usually by a threat or trick, widespread in European and Asian folklore

Death and the Poet – suggested by the line 'The same wind that uproots trees makes the grasses shine' by Rumi, 13th century mystic poet, trans. Coleman Barks with John Moyne, *The Essential Rumi*, Penguin Books, 1995

The Owls That Could Not See Beyond the Ruins – suggested by the line, 'The ruins are as nothing to the hawk perched upon the king's sleeve', again by the poet Rumi. Translator unknown.